SEEING STARS

SEEING STARS

GARY BARWIN

Stoddart Kids
TORONTO • NEW YORK

Published in Canada in 2001 by
Stoddart Kids, a division of Stoddart Publishing Co. Limited
895 Don Mills Road, 400-2 Park Centre, Toronto, Ontario M3C 1W3

Published in the United States in 2002 by
Stoddart Kids, a division of Stoddart Publishing Co. Limited
PMB 128, 4500 Witmer Estates, Niagara Falls, New York 14305-1386

www.stoddartkids.com

To order Stoddart books please contact General Distribution Services
In Canada Tel. (416) 213-1919 Fax (416) 213-1917
Email cservice@genpub.com
In the United States Toll-free tel. 1-800-805-1083
Toll-free fax 1-800-481-6207
Email gdsinc@genpub.com

05 04 03 02 01 1 2 3 4 5

National Library of Canada Cataloguing in Publication Data

Barwin, Gary
Seeing stars

ISBN 0-7737-6227-2

I. Title.
PS8553.A783S43 2001 jC813'.54 C2001-902293-X
PZ7.B288Se 2001

Cover illustration: Murray Kimber
Cover and text design: Tannice Goddard

We acknowledge for their financial support of our publishing program the Canada Council, the Ontario Arts Council, and the Government of Canada through the Book Publishing Industry Development Program (BPIDP).

Printed and bound in Canada

For B.A.A.A. & X

Contents

At my poor house look to behold this night
Earth-treading stars that make dark heaven light.

— SHAKESPEARE (ROMEO & JULIET)

one

Family Math Problem

We were playing poker. I'd set up a chair and a card table beside my mother's bed. I put down a pair of eights. My mother put down a straight in hearts and told me that she'd get out of bed if I found my father.

Sounds simple, like a math problem. If "this" then "that."

Well, here's some more "data":

My father had been gone for twelve years.

My mother had been in bed for twelve years.

You probably don't have to be Einstein to guess that these two facts were connected. I'm certainly not Einstein, either — my hair could never look like that, even if I dropped an entire power station into my bath — but I know that the night my father didn't come home, my mother got into bed and never got up.

I was three.

two

Seeing Stars

I came home late from a rehearsal for *The Wizard of Oz,* the Christmas production that my school was putting on. I was in the "pit orchestra."

"This is the pits," everyone in the band kept saying, even though it was a terrible joke and it was really quite nice to be tucked down there below the stage under all that singing and dancing.

I made a tray of coffee and sandwiches for me and my mom. We hadn't talked about my father in a few days. I backed into the room, pushing the door open with my shoulder.

"You'll never find your father," my mother said matter-of-factly. "I've consulted the stars."

I'd learned from experience that when my mother said

she'd consulted the stars, there was no point arguing. I might as well have tried to spiral-arm wrestle the galaxy. Besides, I knew she really didn't want me to find him. She'd have to get out of bed then. So I changed the subject.

"There's this new girl in my classes," I told her. I put the snack down on the bed. "Her name's Annie. She's from Toronto. She sits beside me in band. Her dad's quite a famous singer."

My mother didn't say anything.

She didn't seem to want to talk about Annie or her father. So we talked about Toto and the Wizard.

"It's funny that it's the dog who figures out the Wizard's just some guy behind a curtain," I said.

"Ah, but the others still believe he can give them what they're looking for," my mother intoned, pretending to be wise.

"Do you think the Wizard had a family back home?" I wondered.

"Wouldn't he have been too old?" my mom said.

"In the movie," I said. "I don't know about the book. It'd be amazing if he had kids, though. Coming home in that big balloon."

She didn't say anything.

I guess dads of any kind weren't her favorite topic.

Big surprise.

It was getting late and so I said good night and turned off the light for her and went to my room — to my computer.

I heard the phone ring.

My mom picked up the phone and began working.

three

Stars By Phone

"Tell me more about your brother." From my bedroom, I could hear my mother talking. She was lying in bed like always and someone had phoned her. She was finding out what they wanted to know and then telling them what the stars said. It was her job.

You'd think that if you were going to ask a question of the stars — even for three dollars a minute — it would be something really important, like, "Is the earth going to survive another hundred years?" "Is there a heaven?" or "How can we feed the hungry?"

But tonight it was pretty much like it always was. At the end of the phone call, and after she'd asked a few questions, she said:

"Yes, you should get a new car, but, Anthony, listen to me. You should keep your girlfriend."

As soon as she'd hung up, the phone rang again. This one was over quickly.

"You should move to Manitoba. Yes. It's quite clear."

It's hard to imagine that things like this would actually have anything to do with the stars, that billions of light-years away, stars are hurrying to get into position to give some guy advice on whether he should buy the latest Bronco or take that job out West. Those are human things.

Like my not knowing about my father. It had nothing to do with the stars — either reading them or wishing on them. Though sometimes I found myself doing a little wishing.

The phone rang again.

And my mom began to ask questions. "How old was she? Was it very far away?" The caller seemed to be quite upset.

"It's OK," my mom said soothingly. "Everything will work out the way it's supposed to."

She was actually quite famous. "Starbright, the star reader" from the TV commercials.

Really she should have been called "Skylight," since that was how she saw the stars.

The commercial began with a close-up of a burning white candle. Then a ringing of little bells and, in a big whoosh, the camera was magically transported to outer space. A woman with a very low breathy voice began speaking as if she was about to cry. "Starlight, Starbright. What does the sky say tonight?" A bunch of numbers that looked like something sparkly was snowing inside of them appeared from nowhere and a voice big as the Death Star, but much more enthusiastic, fired out, "Starbright is waiting to answer your questions, waiting to shine the light of the stars on your life." In small, non-sparkly print at the bottom of the screen: "Only three dollars a minute." My Uncle Barnard had arranged the whole thing when he still worked in advertising. It wasn't exactly my mom's style, but she put up with it. Besides, before that, she'd had me putting up posters all over town.

I don't think she's ever seen the commercial.

My mom ended by telling the upset caller, "It's in the stars. She'll always be with you. Look to the sky and remember."

She put the phone down. I could tell she was upset. I heard it from my desk. It was in her breathing. It sounded forced. I turned off my computer and went to her room.

four

My Mother Planet

Our house was an odd-looking squat one-story. It was covered in a putty-colored plaster and had a flat roof. It looked like a computer CPU housing. That'd make me the central processing unit. And my mother — she'd be the motherboard, of course.

There were only two windows in the whole house. In my room and the spare bedroom. But they had bumpy glass so that you could only see a bit of blurry green for the grass, a smudge of blue for the sky. Sometimes a streak of pink and black when a dog walker went by.

There were skylights above all the other rooms. From what I could figure out from my mother, my father had built the house before he went wherever it was he went to. He must have misread the plans and built the house on its side.

"Mom?" I whispered as I walked into her room. I could hardly see anything. I could just make out my mother lying on her back in the dark.

She didn't look like she belonged in this world.

She looked quite cosmic, really, shaped like a planet or a star. And here I was, as always, checking that she was OK, keeping close to her like a little moon or a satellite, getting her what she needed — food, changes of clothes, books, pens, and paper.

She never left her bed. There were two reasons.

One: she was too large to leave her room. She was even too big to stand up.

Two: she didn't want to.

She had decided to shut out the world. It was as simple as that. When the world didn't turn out to be how she wanted it, she had stayed in bed and tried to become her own world. A different world from the one that contained my father. One where she was never young and hopeful.

She'd escaped out to where there was just the cool light of the stars.

And her big bed.

And a telephone.

And me.

She was like one of those statues of a very fat god. Huge. Immovable. Ready to receive and to give blessings, but not love exactly.

"Everything OK, Mom?" I asked.

Sometimes she got these kinds of upsetting calls.

It didn't surprise me. Anyone could call. And she didn't believe in TV, newspapers, radio, or the Net. All that she knew about the outside world was what she heard on these calls. That and what I told her.

Hardly a representative sample.

The big skylight above her bed was a kind of screen. There was a bit of space on the edge of her bed. I lay down beside her and looked up.

"It's very clear tonight," she said.

We lay there looking up at the sky with the lights turned off. We couldn't hear the cars on the highway, just a few blocks away. There was only the wind making spooky soundtrack sounds through the few scraggly trees in the backyard.

When she was upset she'd often talk about the Zodiac or the constellations.

She didn't believe in them.

"Ridiculous man-made connect-the-dots rubbish," she said. "Those stars have nothing to do with each other. It's nonsense to put them together. Why don't those people know?"

Most callers would talk to her about their zodiac sign.

"The stars aren't like that," she said. It was like she was talking about people in a small village or her high school.

For her the stars had stories, personalities, faces. And you wouldn't put someone from the chess club together with the guys from the football team — a cooling white dwarf together with all those expanding red giants. You'd see the fireworks halfway across the local supercluster. Not that she knew anything scientific about stars. It was all to do with how the stars felt to her.

She always finished her calls by saying what she saw in the stars. When she asked the stars something it was like a big town hall meeting. There's a buzz in the room as the stars talk among themselves. She calls them to order and then certain stars stand up to talk. Some other stars, maybe from a different constellation, jump up and argue, maybe shake their planets at the others.

"Hey, whadda you know? You binary whippersnapper. Wait till you've lived a few billion years like I have."

At the end each star — no matter its size or temperature — gets to vote.

I could see why people would want to phone my mother. If I weren't her son I might phone her. I'd wait till it was dark and the stars were out. I'd dial the sparkly number for "Starbright" and ask where my father was. It'd be great to hear her soft reassuring voice. To feel her quiet certainty. I'd ask if the stars could tell why my father left. And I'd ask her to tell me what she wasn't telling.

I knew that there was something more to her being in bed than just my father leaving. I could feel it. Not in the stars. In my mother.

I must have fallen asleep on the edge of her bed, looking up at the stars. I had a dream I often had. I was just a little kid and my mother, young and skinny, was walking, almost floating, about the house. Her long blonde hair was like many rays of light shining out from her smiling face. Even in the dream I thought this was funny since my mother has always had dark hair. And this woman looked nothing like my mother.

When I woke, my mother was talking on the phone again. I waved good night and slipped away to bed.

five

Toast If I'm Late For School

I woke up the next day to VERY LOUD TWANGY HEARTBREAK.

"SHE LEFT WITH NOTHING EXCEPT A FRYING PAN AND A BUCKET OF TEARS."

Before I even knew where my legs were, or what my name was, some guy in a cowboy hat was yelling fit to stun a bronco.

I turned the clock-radio off.

Ahh.

But I was awake.

I always set my clock radio to a country station because I hate country music. It's the best way to make myself get up. If I set it to anything that I actually liked, I know I'd just lie there listening.

Maybe even fall back to sleep.

I could hear my mom talking quietly on the phone. She must have been working all night. "Go on the boat trip," I thought she was saying.

I started breakfast, brushed my teeth with little kids' bubblegum flavored toothpaste (my favorite), and got dressed. I put on a variation of what I always wear. Khaki pants and a rumpled checked shirt. Lumberjack lite. OK, so it's not the height of fashion, but since everything looks the same, no one can tell if I've done my laundry or if I'm wearing the same things as yesterday or the day before. Or the day before that.

And everything matched.

I quickly ran a brush through my hair, even though it was too short to need brushing. I used to have a burning bush's worth of red hair, so brushing was a habit. But how can you not brush your hair in the morning? It's as natural as — turning on your computer to check your e-mail.

I turned on my computer to check my e-mail.

Nothing.

I helped my mom get ready for the day. I helped her wash and change clothes. I gave her her medication (she had a heart condition because of her size and because she never got out of bed). Then I brought our breakfast in on a tray. I looked at my watch. I was going to miss the bus. I'd set the yelling cowboy to go off as late as possible. I'd only left myself time to shower my left side. Or check my e-mail.

I'd already checked my e-mail. There'd be no time for my left side. And this morning, breakfast would have to have legs. But I was a teenager. I could run with toast in my mouth.

SIX

The Pranks of Curly Haired Varmints

Band was my first class after homeroom.

It was a better way to start the day than doing push-ups or square dancing with Mr. Simmons.

Especially since last class, Mr. Wagner had assigned Annie and me a duet to play on stage for *The Wizard of Oz* production.

We took our saxophones to the practice cubicles at the end of the hall leading to the band room. I had a dented sax from the school's exclusive line of dented saxes. Annie had a lovely old silver one.

"Granddad bought it at a pawn shop. He played in dance bands to make money for law school. Look: his initials." She pointed to a fancy A.C. on the bell.

Annie was amazing. She had long, dark, curly hair and

when I said something to her, she'd look right at me — right into me — with her dark black eyes.

"You think anyone's ever paid their way through music school defending burglars on the weekend?" I asked.

Or at least that's what I meant to say. Instead I ended up saying something like, "I wonder if anyone's ever bugled for burglars, I mean, fluted for felons, or, I mean, being a musician instead of a lawyer. To pay their way through, you know, law school."

Arrgh.

Talking to Annie, I never remembered what I meant say. So I'd speed up, out of control with nerves and say really goofy things. The worst bit was that I couldn't figure out how to stop. Like I was on a runaway train. A runaway train of thought.

About halfway through band period, Annie and I joined the rest of the band. We were the saxophone section.

Indispensable.

Even though she started the term late, Annie could play the band music better than me. She could even play the rests better. We'd have a whole bunch of bars of rest to count while the flutes and clarinets did their thing, and I'd always get mixed up in my counting. Annie would look at me and then hold up her fingers to let me know how many bars were left before we came in again. I'd started relying on her to tell me when to come in.

She must have realized this because when we were playing *The Wizard of Oz* music with the rest of the band, and everyone was playing something really soft, she held up two fingers. I figured that there were only two bars before we came in with these big, loud sforzandos.

Annie and I got ready to play.

Annie and I both took a deep breath so that we could play the loud chords.

Only I came in with the loud sforzando.

The trumpets didn't. The trombones didn't. The guys with the cymbals and drums didn't. There was just me and the very quiet flutes. The rest of the band (and Annie) would have come in in the next bar — the correct place — if they hadn't all been laughing too much to play.

Thanks, Annie.

But in the end I laughed, too. A man's got to count his own rests or fall prey to the pranks of beautiful, curly haired varmints.

seven

Net Fishing

I was hungry when I came back from school.

In the morning, I'd had just enough time to catch the bus. I'd had just enough time to have breakfast (a "dash" of toast.) I'd even had just enough time to have a thought on the way.

It wasn't an Einstein thought.

It was an I-forgot-to-pack-lunch thought.

So when I got home I made two big plates of macaroni and cheese. One for me, one for my mom.

I brought the plate into her room. She was sleeping after being up all night, still holding her half-finished morning cup of coffee. I carefully lifted it out of her sleeping fingers. I pulled the blanket over her, left the macaroni on the night table, and brought the tray full of breakfast dishes back to the kitchen.

I ate in front of my computer. And I did what I did every day after school. I searched for my father.

I searched for him on the Internet — in Usenet, on the World Wide Web, in e-mail lists. I searched for him in message boards. In Yahoo, AltaVista, Google, and all the other search engines. In newsgroups, online telephone directories, and person search databases. In whatever news services I could get into. Anywhere that might have information about my father.

Like one of those guys in the old stories, I set out into the wide world — the World Wide Web — to seek my fortune, to look for my father. So far there'd been no trace of him, but unlike the stars, things change quickly on the Net. And the information wasn't from a hundred million years ago. At least not most of it.

I expected I'd have to face a few giants, maybe e-mail a few princesses stuck in towers, get stuck in a few multiple-user dungeons, and then, at the end of the story, my father's name would show up, and I'd get to meet him. Trumpets and violins play a big, uplifting theme. Closing credits. Happy ending. But it wasn't happening that way. I seemed to be short of a few "worthy swain" ready to point the way toward my father's castle. Of course, it would have helped if he'd been a king.

Or a duke.

Even a movie star.

I wasn't a hacker so I couldn't get into confidential government stuff. Otherwise I could have searched databases of driver's licenses, income tax, even parking tickets and library fines. That'd be kind of funny, finding my father because he owed fifteen cents for an overdue book about training your pet poodle or about modern camouflage. That'd teach him, crouching in the forest with twigs on his hat.

"Hi, Dad, it's Alex — your son." I'd be really casual. "Why don't we take your pet poodle for a walk?"

And he'd have no choice but to get up from his branch lean-to, wipe the green greasepaint from his face, call "Cuddles" out into the forest, and walk with me.

Of course, it's more likely that he's disguised in a blue suit in an office tower in the financial district of some big city. I'd phone him on his cell phone, right in the middle of an important meeting.

Ring. Ring.

"Sorry. I don't know who that could be . . . Who? Alex? I . . ." We'd meet that afternoon at the sandwich place on the first floor of his building. He'd keep stirring his coffee with one of those little orange plastic stir sticks, looking down into it, not wanting to look at me.

One day — around the beginning of rehearsals for *The Wizard of Oz* — I did find a Newton Isaacson on the Net. He was listed in the results of some bridge competition in Florida. I sent an e-mail to the South Florida Bridge Club with the few details I knew. It was the reply to this message that I was checking for.

Five times a day.

eight

Dad Data

I didn't know much about my father. My mother wouldn't talk facts. Well, not beyond the "fact" that "the stars say that he's gone," as if he'd been sucked in by a black hole and because of complicated interstellar physics there was absolutely no possibility that we could ever hear from him again.

A few times I finally did get her talking about him and then she wouldn't stop with these amazing sun-soaked descriptions of how wonderful it all was. If there was a soundtrack, the violins would be going nuts and the oboe would be breaking some serious world records in the international "weepstakes." It was like the whole scene was being looked at from behind the bumpy glass in my room. A bunch of pretty shapes without any clear edges. It was too pretty. It was also too sad, of course.

And something about it didn't quite ring true.

I mean more than how suspiciously well behaved I seemed to have been when I was three.

Here is what data I did have about my dad:

His name was/is Newton Isaacson.

He was born in 1955.

He once lived in the house at 181 Kepler Rd.

He married Marcia Firestone and then they had me.

He left a high-school yearbook that I found in the basement.

It told me that:

He was on the basketball team in high school.

He was a member of the chess club.

He seemed to pick friends who didn't sign their names legibly in high-school yearbooks.

One friend wrote "Have a great 1971, Newt," and then some unreadable scribble that I took to be his name.

The name "Newton" was bad enough, but I wouldn't want to be called Newt. I can just imagine friends high-fiving me and saying, "Hiya, Newt, what's Newt with you?" And my teachers telling each other, "No Newt is good Newt," and yukking it up in the staff room. It's the kind of nickname that makes Bubba sound good. But Newton was an unusual first name. I thought it would make it easier for me to track him down — as long as he hadn't changed it.

Here is what data I *didn't* have about my dad:

Where he was.

Why he left.

What he was doing.

What he looked like.

What it was about him, or what he did, that would make my mother stay in bed for twelve years.

nine

Not Bridge

It was almost six. Time to make supper. I was about to turn off my computer, but instead decided to see what Web pages there were about *The Wizard of Oz.* Maybe I'd find something to impress Annie.

Annie was someone that I wanted to impress.

And not just by getting my tongue run over by an out-of-control train of thought or being hassled by the toughs at school.

I went to the kitchen to get myself a root beer. I sat down at the computer and snapped open the can.

Yes! There was a message from the South Florida Bridge Club.

To: alexisaacson@hotmail.com
From: SFTrumps@sunalways.net
Subject: Re: My Father

Alex:
I am sorry to disappoint you but the Newton Isaacson in our club is twenty years old. Too young to be your father. I printed out your e-mail and showed it to him. He asked me to tell you that he wishes you luck with your search. And also to let you know that as far as he knows, you two are not related. Best wishes. We hope you find your father.

Sincerely,
Doris Tamana
Vice President
South Florida Bridge Club ("The Trumps")

I've said it before, but I'll say it again.

Arrgh.

It was time to visit Uncle Barnard. I needed some new leads.

I brought some cheese sandwiches in for my mom.

"I'll be back soon. Then I'll make something proper for dinner."

ten

Without Gloves

Even though he lived just across the city, I didn't see my Uncle Barnard very often. He'd come over to our house every now and then to share in one of our sumptuous feasts. Maybe pork and beans from a can, lovingly warmed up in the microwave and splendidly presented by our team of loyal servants, each perfectly dressed in a black tuxedo, white gloves, and a sash in our family's colors.

OK. So I'd bring the pork and beans into my mother's room on a tray. But Uncle Barnard didn't care. He'd plunk himself down in a chair beside my mother and wait to be issued a spoon and a bowl. Or a shovel and a pitchfork. Uncle Barnard was not interested in how we folded the serviettes. He just wanted to eat.

He was very tall and thin. He'd make these crazy

gestures with his long, spindly arms. Like a windmill having a fit. And unless you're a farmer with a really big bag of grain, who'd want to visit a windmill that acts like it's just been stung by a bee? The truth was, I was kind of scared of my uncle.

But now I'd decided that it was time, like Don Quixote, to joust at this windmill, to ask him about my father.

I figured out where my uncle's apartment was. Though I couldn't find my father, it was easy to look up Uncle Barnard on the Net and even get a map of where he lived. It would take two buses: 52 and 3. The 3 didn't come for ages. When it finally did, I had to do some archaeology to find the transfer. It was in my back pocket alongside an ancient piece of gum and the jawbone of a saber-toothed tiger. The bus pulled onto Uncle Barnard's street. I stepped out and began walking.

The apartment building was at the very end of the street. There was a buzzer system, but the door had been propped open with a chipped piece of wood, so I just walked up the one flight of stairs to my uncle's and knocked on the door. I didn't use his doorknocker. It was a large and none-too-fresh fish tied to the door by its tail. I suppose it discouraged visitors, even usually persistent door-to-door salesmen. Except those with rubber gloves and no sense of smell.

Uncle Barnard flung the door open.

"I would have called . . ." I began.

"Don't have a phone," Uncle Barnard said, swooping his arms around. "What'd I need it for? Chatting with the operator? Ordering pizza?" He looped his arm around, motioning me to come in.

"Nice fish," I said, pointing at the doorknocker.

"A perch," he said proudly. "Last month it was a mackerel."

It was obvious that normal behavior and Uncle Barnard didn't get along. Normal behavior kept banging on Uncle Barnard's door trying to sell him a normal life and Uncle Barnard kept peering through the peephole, telling it to go away. Maybe it had kept coming back until he hung up the mackerel. I guess normal behavior doesn't wear gloves.

Uncle Barnard's living room was at the end of a long hall. It was filled with books. There was a large aquarium in the corner. In the center of the room was an easel. There was a huge painting sitting on it. It was of a frog painting a picture. The frog's picture was of a frog painting a picture of a frog painting. This frog was painting a picture of a frog painting. And THAT frog was painting a picture of a frog painting. And so on. It kept going until the frogs and the paintings were extremely tiny. It was as if the paintings were ripples circling out from some molecule-sized frog painting in the center. Like the ripples a tiny frog would make jumping into a pond. I felt I was looking down from somewhere high up, about to fall into the painting.

"Been working on that for a long time now," Uncle Barnard said. "Started before I left the agency."

"It's . . . nice," I said. "You like frogs?" I know. It was a pretty silly thing to say to someone who has spent years painting an incredibly detailed picture of frogs. But what else do you say to someone who has spent years painting such an incredibly detailed picture of frogs?

"Once I had a dream about a giant frog," he said. "It flew out of the sky and I climbed onto its back. It took me flying up into the clouds. And I felt happy. Very happy." He was waving his arms up and down like they were wings — giant frog wings. "That, too, was before I left the agency. And before . . ." He became still for a moment.

"Uncle Barnard?" I said.

"And then I left. But I kept working on this picture," he said abruptly. "Now how's your mother?"

"Good. She gets lots of calls. From the ad."

"Tea," he said. "We need some tea," and he went clattering off.

I followed him into the kitchen. There were pots and pans and hammers and saws and many other kinds of tools that I couldn't identify. Somewhere from all this jumble, Uncle Barnard produced a teapot and two chipped cups. He had one of those big old Russian water heaters — a samovar, I think they're called — sitting on a burner. He filled the teapot with steaming water and plopped in two lint-covered teabags that he took from his shirt pocket. Considering the look of Uncle Barnard's shirt, I wasn't sure that I'd drink tea made from those teabags.

We walked back and sat down at Uncle Barnard's table.

"Uncle," I began. "I want to know about my father. I want to know what happened to him."

"It was . . . Your . . ." Uncle Barnard's eyebrows were joined together over the bridge of his nose. This monobrow began to bunch up like a nervous caterpillar. Then my uncle stood up suddenly. "Just remembered," he said. "Got to meet a man about a frog. We must talk another time." He strode down the hall and began to wrestle with a huge coat. Then he was out the door and I was alone in his apartment with the fish, the steaming teapot, and the pictures of the frogs that made me feel like I was falling.

"Guess I'll have to talk to Uncle Barnard another time," I said to no one in particular.

And they didn't answer.

On the way out, I stopped and looked at some of the books on Uncle Barnard's shelf.

There were books of strange-looking poetry. Books about Siberia, about Fiji, about Iceland. About astrology. About painting. Lots of books about fishing — some very old-looking ones with detailed drawings about hooks and fish. Books about frogs. And there was a whole shelf of books about airplanes. It looked like Uncle Barnard wanted to learn to fly. I pulled a battered book off the shelf. I was sure that Uncle Barnard wouldn't miss it — or mind that I borrowed it. A little reading to help me avoid crashing into mountains on the flight-simulator program that I had at home. I stuck the book in my coat pocket and closed the perch-knockered door behind me.

eleven

Alfa Tango Mike

On the way home I stopped at the bank machine. A check had arrived that morning from the Psychic Phone Network. That's the company that took care of billing the people who phoned my mother. The checks arrived each month, and my mother signed them and gave them to me to deposit. I used to go to the bank with a little note from my mom "telling" the tellers how much money to give me back. I hated how the tellers would look at me as if they knew something.

Maybe they did.

Or maybe it was just because they were sitting on the side of the counter where the money was.

Anyway, the bank machine never looked at me funny.

And I could make the joke about how I'm putting money for the fortune-teller into the fortune-teller.

I didn't say it was a good joke.

There was a lineup at the bank machine so I opened up Uncle Barnard's flying book. It was full of great words like "yaw" and "aileron" and many complicated charts.

There were also a couple of pages on the pilot's alphabet. I figured out that my name would be Alfa Lima Echo X-ray.

Annie's sounded nicer: Alfa November November India Echo.

Someone had written little notes in pen in the margins of the book and had underlined various sentences. There was also a handwritten note on a folded piece of paper between the pages about the pilot's alphabet.

The line at the Alfa Tango Mike hadn't moved at all. I think the man at the machine was doing the entire year's banking for India Bravo Mike. He had little piles of paper and envelopes organized all around him. I had some time, so I unfolded the note and began reading:

Barn,
We can do it. She'll be ready soon.
Let the fun begin!
Meet me at the Quarry at five.
— N

Barn was probably Uncle Barnard. What about N?

Newton?

This was a note from my father! A note to his brother. A serious lead.

Now, what did it mean?

"Hey. This ain't a library!"

What?

Oh, yes.

Translation: It was my turn to use the bank machine. The guy in line behind me was getting impatient. This wasn't road rage. It was line rage.

So I'll bank.

After I'd made the deposit, I ran for the bus. I was excited. This time while I ran for the bus, I had time for many thoughts.

I realized that I'd never seen my father's handwriting or read his words before. Not that I understood them. But now I had something more to ask Uncle Barnard about. What was it they could do? Who was this "she" that would soon be ready? Even though whatever it was happened years before the Net, maybe I could at least find out about the quarry. Now that I thought about it, there was more chance of finding something on the Net than trying to surf Uncle Barnard's frog-infested memory banks.

And, besides, my computer had a more attractive interface.

"You need to give your daughter love. This is a difficult time for her. Don't make her grow up too fast." My mother was on the phone with a caller when I got home. The last thing I wanted to do was to make us supper, but I was a growing boy after all, and my mom couldn't read the stars on cheese sandwiches alone.

So spaghetti it was then. I turned the radio on to the jazz station — Charlie Parker was wailing on "How High the Moon" — and began cutting onions.

twelve

Secret Mother

I hadn't told anyone about my mother, but everyone seemed to know — at least about her size. At school the teachers gave me worried looks like I was a puppy left too long in a hot car. No one seemed to know about the star reading or that she was "Starbright."

And I didn't fill them in.

Kids had been lobbing verbal grenades at me for years. I wasn't in a hurry to give them more ammunition.

Once when I got on the bus near the beginning of the term, Bud Loftyear said in a really loud voice, "When she sits around the house, she really sits around the house," and made a big show of slapping his knee and elbowing Matt Stone. They both pretended to be totally cracked up about it. Cracked up like someone hit them in the head with a school bus and their brains dribbled out, if you ask me.

They were looking right at me the whole time, as if to say, "We can do this to you and you can't stop us."

They had a point.

There was nothing I could do. Not unless some friendly superhero just happened to be flying by or the Wizard of Oz gave me a little bag full of Great Strength. Maybe Toto could bite their ankles.

Or rip their curtains open.

They kept looking at me to see if they'd got to me. Of course, they had, but I did my best not to let on. I just sat down beside Eleanor Knowles and pretended to be fantastically interested in my watch. Eleanor didn't want to get involved. She was, it seemed, herself suddenly fantastically interested in the view out the window. And who could blame her: telephone poles, convenience stores, broad stretches of mesmerizing pavement. A trip down the Nile would be a disappointment after that. Myself, I think I would rather face crocs who at least attack YOU when they want to hurt you, instead of your mother.

After that it became a kind of code. Bud and Matt could just make a little slap to their knee or mouth the word "house" and I'd know what they meant. Like the kind of Japanese court drama we'd learned about in drama class where a raised eyebrow can mean a lot, except that this was hardly high art, though it may have been an ancient tradition — the old back-of-the-bus toughs torment the son of Fat Lady.

So the morning after I had visited Uncle Barnard, I wasn't exactly overjoyed when I got on the bus and there, near the front, were Matt and Bud, their faces carpeted with ear-to-ear spite.

"Hey, Alex," Bud jeered. "*House* your mother?"

"Yeah, she just *hanging* around?" Matt added. "Or is she out running a marathon?"

"Maybe she's running after his dad," Bud said.

They both started slapping their knees and yukking it up.

OK.

There comes a time when you've got to decide whether you're going to be a Munchkin or a Lion.

As it turned out, I decided to be, well, if not the Lion, then at least the Tin Man on a very bad day. I didn't have an ax. But I did have my saxophone case. I held it up at shoulder level. I walked quickly by Matt and slammed the case right across the side of his head.

Wham.

Matt fell against the seat. He was bleeding from his temple.

The bus driver stopped the bus with a jerk. Then she started yelling. I dropped the saxophone case, ran to the front of the bus, and pulled the big handle that opened the doors. I ran down the stairs and onto the sidewalk. I kept running.

OK.

So maybe I was the Scarecrow.

I was certainly acting like I had no brain. And I was going to need Glinda the Good Witch to help get me out of this one.

thirteen

Well-Adjusted Zinger

So I'd just clobbered someone on the school bus. Then I'd taken off. Going to school was out of the question.

But I also couldn't go home. My mom wasn't THAT out of touch that she wouldn't notice if I were home on a school day.

I didn't know what to do. Up to now, my biggest school mess-up was coloring outside of the lines. And that was in kindergarten. Well, OK, once last year in grade nine I was told to redo a project about South America because I'd copied most of it straight from an encyclopedia that I'd found on the Net.

But none of these were big deals.

Bashing someone with — a weapon — my saxophone case . . .

That was a big deal.

I wanted to run away. To never go back to school. To hop on a bus and keep traveling.

It wasn't fight or flight.

It was fight *and* flight.

In the principal's brain, they'd take down the big gold plaque saying "GOOD KID" and replace it with a poster of me with the headline: "WANTED for saxophone assault and truancy."

I wondered if they would suspend me.

Probably.

Worse, they might call the police and have me charged. They were always talking about "zero tolerance" in our school.

But they'd have to find me first.

Where should I go?

I walked a little, not really knowing where I was walking except not into traffic or telephone poles. And even that was an effort.

Something had changed when I hit Matt. Up till now, I had been able to balance my mother, my crazy uncle, the search for my father, and the normal childhood I thought I deserved. But this was the straw that tipped the camel over, that messed up the balance. I'd had enough. I wished a cyclone would just yank me up and plunk me down someplace that wasn't Kansas. Sure it'd be nice if it was multicolored and full of magic, but that wasn't necessary. And I wouldn't ask the Wizard to take me home again.

I ended up making my way toward Annie's house. I wasn't planning to — my feet just took me there.

I'd been there once before, or at least to the mailbox, to

drop off some music for Annie. Annie lived with both her parents, but her dad was a singer and was "on the road" a lot, touring with his own band, so Annie sometimes didn't see him for a month at a time.

"But he comes home eventually, right?" I'd said to Annie.

"Yes," she had to admit. "He usually brings me back something interesting. He feels bad to be away. Last month he was down south and he brought me a Navaho bead necklace."

I'd be happy to have the father, even without the soundtrack or jewelry.

Annie told me that her dad had promised to take her on tour with him one day. That sounded like an amazing idea.

Annie's mother worked at the local newspaper, the *Kensington Star*. I didn't know exactly what she did, but I knew that she and Annie got along well. Annie had said that "she's pretty cool, actually" and told me about their midnight picnics by the river.

I arrived at Annie's door, out of breath, and rang the bell. Annie's mother answered. At least, I guessed it was her.

Unless, of course, it was a burglar. But how many burglars answer the door? And in sandals? Burglars don't wear sandals. It'd be unprofessional. She looked a bit hippyish the way some librarians do — her hair tied back with a scarf, a jean skirt, silver earrings, bracelets, and rings that were probably from India. I could see where Annie got her dark eyes and dark curly hair.

"Annie's at school." She had an American accent.

"I'm a friend of Annie's," I said, though she'd obviously already figured that out. Of course, Annie was at school.

"Why don't you come in anyway?" Annie's mother said.

I must have looked confused. "Maybe you'd like some tea. I've just made some."

She put two earthenware mugs down beside a little teapot. "It's Red Zinger," she said. "Do you like it?"

This wasn't Uncle Barnard's tea. It wasn't the tea I made in the cup with hot water from the tap for my mom and me. This was well-adjusted tea.

"Are you OK?" Annie's mom asked.

I wasn't OK. And though I felt relieved to be sitting down in a well-adjusted kitchen with Annie's well-adjusted mother, I still had no idea what I was going to do.

She was easy to talk to, though. I ended up explaining what had happened. I was surprised I told her. It's not exactly the best way to impress a girl's mother — describing how you bashed someone. She didn't seem disturbed by what I said. She even smiled when I told her that I'd used my saxophone case.

"So what happens now?" she asked in a quiet voice. "Have you spoken to your parents?"

My mother! It'd be all right for me to be gone during the day. I usually was — when I was at school. I always left a supply of food and water beside her bed when I went out. But she'd need me home after school. How long was I going to hide out? I'd have to return home and go back to school eventually. Wouldn't I?

I didn't really want to tell Annie's mother about my mom, but somehow it just came out, not exactly the truth, but more or less the truth. I said that my mom was sick, that she was "confined to bed." My father, I said, didn't live with us. This was more than I wanted to say.

"OK," Annie's mom said. She said it as if she had all the time in the world. As if there was time for everything. And there wasn't a trace of judgment in it.

"So you need to tell your mother. She's going to find out anyway." She took a sip of tea. "But she's sick, and you don't want to upset her." Pause. "You could explain to the school how difficult it's been looking after her. You could explain how you felt."

I'd rather have served time chained to the wall of a rat-infested dungeon beside treacherous brigands than tell the school about my mother. The Wizard of Oz hid behind a curtain. He didn't want anyone to know that he was really an old guy from Omaha.

As I figured it, what the school didn't know couldn't hurt me.

We didn't say anything for a while, just sat there sipping our tea.

"So you need to think about what to do," Annie's mom said eventually. She told me her name was Clare. "Well, I don't have to go into work until later, and I was planning to do some yard work. Why don't you help me?"

The backyard was huge. It must have looked amazing in the summer. Flowers everywhere. There were nooks with benches to sit on. There was a pond with some lilies floating in the thick green water. Probably frogs when it was warm out. Uncle Barnard's frog painting flickered into my mind and I felt like I was falling.

"Here," Clare said, handing me a rake. "You start over there."

There's nothing that makes you notice trees so much as

holding a rake. And this yard was full of trees. Big creaking oak and maple trees. The ground was covered with their leaves.

I'd never raked before. There was only one tree in our little yard, and I'd always just left its leaves on the ground. I was the only one who ever went into the yard anyway. Well, except for squirrels, and they didn't seem to care.

I liked raking. It was nice out. The sky was . . . sky blue, there was only a wispy breeze, and the air was just a little sharp. Every now and then a wave of panic went through me, but it was hard to keep it up while raking. And Clare was at the other end of the yard, raking in long flowing movements, like a slow dance. It was hard to get too panicked beside someone who seemed so calm, so quietly happy. I could see where Annie got it from, though being fifteen she wasn't quite so calm.

I could also understand why Annie always came home for lunch. The cafeteria was like an earthquake compared to this.

And what *would* Annie say when she came home and saw me raking the leaves with her mom? I mean I didn't even know Annie that well to begin with, let alone her mother. But Clare didn't seem to mind and so I kept raking, filling about ten bags of leaves before I'd finished my section of the yard.

I was hoping that Clare might tell me what to do. It'd be easier than having to make my own decision.

Finally, to get her talking, I said, "I'm going to have to face the music some time."

Clare was leaning on her rake, looking up into a tree. "Yes," she said simply. "That's true." Then she pointed high up into the tree where some squirrels were making a nest. She watched them silently for a few moments.

I felt a wave of panic. She wasn't going to make this easy for me. I began raking again, a little more enthusiastically than I'd meant to.

"Alex," she said after a few minutes of my furious gardening. "You're still upset." She paused. "Maybe you'll feel calmer tomorrow." I stopped raking and looked at the ground, embarrassed by my little lawn-care outburst. Clare scanned the yard. "Perhaps there's something you could do for me this afternoon," she said.

I had no idea what she was going to suggest. Duking it out with the flowerbeds? More World Leaf-Wrestling Federation action?

"There are some pilots coming to the convention center — there's a meeting of the local Aeronautical Society this week — and I wonder if you'd like to interview one of them for the paper? They come from all over, and there's a few real interesting ones. I was just on the phone this morning with someone I met last year. Chuck Ambersoll, a very nice fellow. He's a pilot and an inventor and he used to be an instructor for the Air Force. He'd be an excellent person to interview. I could call up now and arrange a time for you to meet him, if you'd like?"

A pilot and an inventor sounded cool, but I'd never interviewed anyone before. "I've never interviewed anyone before."

"Not to worry. I'll help you. We often include interviews by students in the Weekend section. Besides, Annie told me about that funny article you did for the music department's website."

Oh, yes, *that* article. "Why Every Teacher Should Skydive (or Play Tuba in the Band)." Another piece of evidence in the principal's "Alex" file. But my English marks weren't that bad. And many people did tell me that they liked the article. Besides, Annie's mom said she'd help. And, if I wrote something for Annie's mom, maybe I'd get a chance to spend more time with Annie. Maybe it'd be something to save this whole thing from being a complete mess-up.

In any case, I'd found almost no useful "facts" in the search for my father. I could trick Uncle Barnard into talking about the note by dazzling him with what I learned from the pilot.

I'd make this part of my fiendishly clever master plan.

When I came up with one.

fourteen

Homeward Bounce

"Hi, Mom, I'm home." Annie was at the back door, home for lunch. "Alex!"

"There's no place like home, there's . . . Wait, where's Toto?" I pretended to look around.

"Alex is helping with some yard work." Clare walked over and kissed Annie on the cheek.

"But what about school . . . the bus . . . ?"

"It's lunchtime," Clare said. "Let's find something to eat."

As we walked in, Annie said in a low voice, "No one can believe it. You hitting Matt."

"Mild-mannered saxophone player in class, wild saxophone-wielding fiend on bus," I joked. My new role as fiend seemed to agree with me. For once I seemed to be able to out-talk that speeding train of thought and leave my mumble-mouth behind.

"No one should insult someone like that — or their mother. He deserved it," Annie said with emphasis. "Everyone thinks so."

"Except Matt and the principal." I drew my finger across my throat like a knife.

"Lunch." Clare motioned to the table where there were a number of clay bowls filled with various kinds of paste, each a different shade of brown. There was also some bread and a jug of juice. She passed Annie and me a plate. "Tahini, hummus, baba ganoush. They're good. Really."

Annie and her mother dug right in. I tried a bit of the baba ganoush. It tasted a bit musty, but good. The juice was carrot juice, which was sweet and tart at the same time. My body was telling me that this stuff was better than baloney sandwiches and mac and cheese, which I ate all too often. Still, though, I'd miss baloney sandwiches if I were to give them up. And, besides, food with no nutrition reminded me of . . . messing about with computers.

Some people get a kind of itch inside them and begin to hanker for junk food. I was beginning to itch. It had been hours since I'd last checked my e-mail.

Annie laughed at me, but led me to her parents' study where there was a computer in the middle of piles of paper and CDs. And I thought that there were a lot of leaves to rake!

"My dad," Annie smiled. "Not the neatest of disorganized, long-haired touring musicians."

There were two messages waiting for me.

The first promised me help with my mortgage.

"Yes, the payments on my place in the south of France are killing me!" I held my hand across my forehead and looked worried.

"Not to mention the simply smashing private jet," Annie said in an English accent as she read over my shoulder.

The second message was very strange. It said:

From: bounce@bounce.net
To: alexisaacson@hotmail.com
Subject: Bouncing

Even if this message doesn't bounce, it is a bouncing message.

That was it. I had no idea who it was from or what they were trying to tell me. I knew what it meant for a message to bounce. When you sent an e-mail to an incorrect address, it got bounced back. But what did they mean by a "bouncing message"?

Annie laughed when she read it. "It sounds like it's from Tigger, you know, from Winnie-the-Pooh — bouncy, pouncy, and all that other springy stuff."

While I was online (and while Annie left to gather some books to bring back to school), I did a quick check to see if a new listing had turned up for my father.

It had!

I found a listing for an nisaacson@bikevertical.net in a mountain biking newsgroup. N for Newton?

I wrote and asked:

To: Nisaacson@bikevertical.net
From: alexisaacson@hotmail.com
Subject: My Father

My name is Alex Isaacson. I am 15 and I have been looking for my father. His name is Newton Isaacson. He has no middle name. Is this you? I found your name in a mountain biking newsgroup. My mother's name is Marcia Isaacson-Firestone.

If it's not you, then, from one Isaacson to another, sorry.

Alex Isaacson

Annie came back in the room and flopped down in the chair beside mine, her arms full of library books. "Did you send a reply to Tigger?"

I was just able to close my message before she could see it.

"I was trying to think of something clever," I said. That would explain why I was taking so long!

"So what did you come up with?"

I began typing:

From: alexisaacson@hotmail.com
To: bounce@bounce.net
Subject: Re: Bouncing

The message didn't bounce, though its meaning did.

Maybe you could explain on the rebound.

-Alex "Bounce for Glory" Isaacson

"Ugh!" Annie said and she was right. There are enough bad puns in the world without making up new ones.

But I couldn't help myself.

It's like eating too many peanuts. You know you shouldn't, you know you're going to end up with a sick feeling, but you just can't stop.

It was time for Annie to go back to school. We found Clare in the backyard, reading. She'd called the pilot. We were to meet at Gerry's Village Restaurant. She slipped a piece of paper out of her book and handed it to me. It was a list of guidelines for students conducting interviews for the Weekend section. There were also a few basic questions for me to ask my "interviewee." I thanked Clare for lunch and she said, "Anytime." It sounded like she meant it.

I walked Annie to the corner and then headed back along King Street toward Gerry's.

fifteen

Crash Course

It took me about half an hour to get to the restaurant. I'd stopped and bought a notebook, which I imagined a big-time reporter would use. I sat up at the counter, put my notebook down, and ordered. I didn't go to Gerry's often, but I'd been a few times when I just had to get out of the house.

They made these awesome old-fashioned milkshakes.

There was a man sitting on the stool beside me drinking coffee and reading a newspaper. He looked up and smiled.

It seemed to be just a normal smile, not a "what-are-you-doing-out-of-school-and-why-did-you-clobber-that-kid-with-your-saxophone-case?" kind of smile.

So I said "Hi," trying to make it sound like it was a normal "hi" and not an "I'm-out-of-school-and-I-don't-know-why-I-clobbered-him-with-my-saxophone-case" kind of hi.

"Chuck Ambersoll," he said. "You must be . . ."

"Alex."

"So you work for the paper," he said, motioning to my notebook. "You don't go to school during the day?"

I was sure he was just joking, but I didn't know how much Clare had told him. Right then I felt like I was about to nose-dive to the ground. Free-fall. I felt panicky again. I still did go to school . . . didn't I? I didn't know what I was going to do, though. Guys like Matt and Bud had experience with talking to principals and police about "certain events," but not me.

The Munchkins were pretty happy that Dorothy clobbered the witch. I didn't expect that the principal would be so happy about Matt. But then again, how much could the principal or the police do? There were kids who did much worse things all the time. And with real weapons. I expected that they'd suspend me for a few weeks or so. But whatever happened in school, I knew that I'd have to deal with Matt outside.

"I do go . . . well, except for today, I had a bit of a problem . . . but generally, during the day . . . I mean during the weekdays . . . I do attend . . . I do go to school, though not today," I finally said.

Chuck smiled. "And why not?" He rested his chin on his hand and looked quizzical. He wasn't going to lose the opportunity of making me squirm.

Here goes.

"I kind of had a problem on the bus, a run in, I hit . . . I'm laying low for a while," I said.

Right, Alex. Nice one. Laying low for a while. Maybe you should tie up your horse and head for the saloon.

"An unscheduled holiday. I see." For a few moments, Chuck looked like he was thinking hard. "All right, so you've encountered some difficulty and so you're on holiday for today," he finally said. He was letting me go. The cat had released the mouse so that it could scurry back to the safety of its own little hole in the wall. "At least there's no trouble now. Clare said that you were a good kid and I believe her. So now I guess you want to know everything about me, right?"

"Everything," I said, opening up my notebook purposefully and hiding Clare's student guidelines sheet behind it. I was a big-time reporter after all.

Chuck took a sip of his coffee and put his newspaper down on the seat beside him. "OK, then," he said, gathering his thoughts. He had meant to give me a hard time. It had been some kind of test.

"I grew up in the Midwest, in Wichita," he began. "In a very ordinary family. When I was eleven, my father was sent out to Korea. He was shot down and shipped back in a box. I took that pretty hard, as you can imagine. I was kind of lost for a while," he said. "Like you, I encountered some difficulties, but I stayed out of serious trouble . . . more or less.

"Then an old Air Force buddy of my father's got me interested in flying. Took me up a whole bunch of times and I got the flying bug. It was in my blood, anyway, my dad having been in the service. Eventually, I joined the Air Force and I've been flying planes ever since. It straightened me right out. When I was sent to Vietnam, I didn't have time to mess up or feel sorry for myself. I was in the air, shooting at the enemy, dropping bombs, saving my country. And, as they say," Chuck smiled, "as long as you follow orders you can do what you want."

I couldn't imagine it. Hitting Matt was enough of a big deal for me, let alone dropping bombs to save my country.

I asked him about how he got started as an inventor.

"When I was in Vietnam, and I wasn't that much older than you, I had the bright idea that if "personnel decelerators"— parachutes — could be attached to men, they could also be attached to planes, even big mama jets. Ever since then, I've worked on developing this parachute idea. When a plane starts to go down, the pilot just yanks on a lever, a bunch of chutes are released, and the plane lands soft as cottonwool. A lot of lives can be saved. And when you consider the cost of a crashed jet — what with all the lawyers at work — a bunch of twisted metal gets very expensive. My parafoils can save lives and money at the same time. Some of the crash deaths that have happened in this city could have been avoided."

Everyone who lives here knows that Kensington, Ontario, is famous for plane crashes. Every few years it seems, some famous person has a plane crash here. Recently — and for obvious reasons, there were lots of jokes about it — Fallingstar's private jet had crashed into the lake. The entire band had to swim to safety. There had been a plane carrying a congressman and a soccer team from Brazil that had slammed into the ground. It's supposedly something to do with the escarpment, the distance above sea level, and the fog that comes off the lake.

"Like that crash that's supposed to have happened ten,

twelve years ago," Chuck continued. "Actually, it's almost exactly the anniversary of when the crash is supposed to have occurred. Did you hear about it?" Chuck sounded very excited. "The story is that there was a kid who tried to fly this crazy homemade plane with two guys dressed up in ridiculous costumes. They made up crazy names for themselves."

"It sounds sort of . . . familiar," I said. If I'd heard anything, I remembered nothing at all about it, but (a) I didn't want him to think that I knew nothing, and (b) he sounded so enthusiastic, it seemed like he was about to tell me an entire novel about it and I'd heard enough about strange people just being part of my own strange family.

"Well, the crash wouldn't have happened if they'd had some of my parafoils on the plane. The plane apparently took a nosedive and buried itself right into the end of some poor sap's driveway."

"Did it hit anyone?" I thought of Dorothy's house landing on top of the witch in *The Wizard of Oz*.

"No. At least not as far as anyone knows. Whoever lived at the end of that driveway must have been lucky." Chuck took another sip of his coffee. "I said I've got the flying bug, but I also have an interest in what goes wrong. I've always been fascinated by crashes like that one, where all anyone knows is rumors and stories. I collect all the information I can about them. In fact, right now I'm researching the exact crash I was just telling you about."

I was sure that there were a lot of questions I should have been asking, but I was too busy scribbling like mad in my notebook, trying to keep up with what Chuck was saying. I didn't have time to probe deep into Chuck's airborne soul, or the soul of the student guidelines.

"You know, Alex," Chuck said looking at his watch. "I have to go down to the airplane museum to meet an old friend and look over some planes. Why don't we finish the interview there? I'd reckon it's a lot more interesting than this coffee shop."

We'd meet at the entrance to the museum in an hour. He had to get going.

"Three o'clock then. Just ask for Chuck Ambersoll at the front desk."

sixteen

Airlined Paper

There were a few ducks swimming under me as I walked across the King Street bridge. There was a large man sitting on a bench looking over the river. He would rip a page out of a big book and fold it into a paper plane. Then he'd launch the plane across the river. All of the planes ended up in the river and were carried away by the current as they began to sink. One of them just missed a duck. One almost made it across, but ended up downstream like all the others.

The man patiently repeated the process again and again. Ripping out a page from the book (hadn't he heard of loose-leaf paper?), he would carefully fold it, using the book on his knees as a table. Then he'd toss the plane toward the river. He wasn't very energetic. He tossed the planes like he didn't really care. He twirled his hand about, following the spiraling descent of the planes into the water, as if he was trying to hurry up the inevitable. His twirling hand was like a whirligig, or a little windmill in a weak wind . . . a windmill?

Uncle Barnard? It was Uncle Barnard.

"Uncle Barnard!" I yelled and waved my arms. But the traffic on King Street was loud and he didn't notice me. It was a long walk around to the riverbank and I didn't want to be late for Chuck Ambersoll, especially since my fiendishly clever master plan included my stint as a star reporter for the *Kensington Star*.

So I left Uncle Barnard to try to set the record for what must surely have been the first trans-river crossing by a paper airplane set by a grown man.

Unless he had gone down to the river to see that man about a frog . . .

seventeen

Bound To Oz

"Isaacson, eh?" The security guard looked at my ID with suspicion. I'd had to bang on the doors in order to be let in. The museum wasn't normally open on Tuesdays.

"I'm here to see Chuck Ambersoll."

"Ambersoll, eh?" the guard said thoughtfully. He looked at my ID card. "Isaacson, eh?"

"Yes . . ."

"Ambersoll, eh?" he said.

"Yes."

He tilted my ID card and looked at it curiously. "Isaacson, eh?"

"Yes!"

The guard paused a moment, clearly thinking deeply. Countries would rise and fall based on his actions. Planets would set their orbits based on his instructions. Finally the guard said, "Ambersoll, eh?"

"Yes!!" I said. Then added for good measure, "Sir."

But before we started another round of "Isaacson/ Ambersoll, eh?" Chuck Ambersoll walked up to the desk, accompanied by an older man with wisps of white hair sticking out of his almost bald head.

"Alex, this is Dr. Tycho." Dr. Tycho shook my hand vigorously.

"Dr. Tycho was just telling me that he knew an Isaacson from around here who used to fly," Chuck said. "Maybe he's related to you."

"Yah, yah. Barnard. Barnard Isaacson was his name," Dr. Tycho said. "But I haven't seen him for years."

This was one of the kinds of coincidences that my mother would say was "in the stars." Lately, a lot of things seemed like the stars were pulling the strings — if I believed in the stars.

But I didn't tell them that Barnard was my uncle.

Today I'd seen him flying paper airplanes. Never mind flying *real* airplanes, Uncle Barnard couldn't even get his paper airplanes across the river. I was hardly going to tell them the good news. Anyway, Uncle Barnard and my mother were my secret. Still, it surprised me to hear that Uncle Barnard ever could fly. With his spinning arms, it'd be like having the propeller inside the airplane.

"Let's go look at the planes," Chuck Ambersoll said. We walked into the main hangar where there was a display of old warplanes. "Dr. Tycho and I share an interest in plane crashes. We each have filing cabinets full of information."

"Yah, yah. It is true. We have been talking about the

story of the kid, we think it was a girl, who tried to fly a crazy plane across the country with a man some people say was her father, and another man. The plane was specially built, a very strange design, I'm told. It crashed here."

"How old was she? Did she die?"

"No one knows what happened. Or any of the details. But people talk sometimes . . ."

"The girl was about ten, we think. We've both been on a mission to know everything about it, right, Dr. Tycho?"

"Yah. Yah. We've heard they dressed up in fancy costumes. Thought they were superheroes or something or other. They didn't even file a flight plan."

"Do you have to do that?" I asked.

"Of course. Yah, yah. Of course."

"The fact that the whole thing was so unusual, and that no one even knows who they were, is part of the fun," Chuck said.

"Fun, indeed," said Dr. Tycho. "And just today we've located some new information. There's a man by the name of Nicholas Copper. He used to be a flyer from around here but he has moved out to Alberta. Some people say that he knows about the flight. Maybe he was one of the men onboard. Well, today we have found out where he lives. Good, no?"

"And I'm going to fly out to see him," Chuck said. "Tonight."

As we spoke, we'd been walking around the planes in the hangar. Many of the planes in the museum were small fighter planes from the First and Second World Wars. They were painted bright yellow and had the Royal Canadian

Air Force insignia on them. There was a Spitfire that I could get in. It was much smaller in the cockpit than I expected. Being inside was like being in a cocoon . . . or like being in a bathtub with wings. Chuck slid the windshield over the cockpit. Everything became silent. I could imagine flying high in the blue sky above the fields of Europe, scanning the air for other planes, scouring the ground for signs of activity. I could see why planes were often named after birds. I felt that my eyes would become like the eyes of a hawk or an eagle, penetrating the thin air.

Then Chuck took me over to a large, dark-green bomber, the kind with little glass bubbles and machine guns sticking out on the front and back of the plane. It was a castle on wheels. It was a surprise to realize that many of the controls worked without electronics. Some things were made of leather or with metal rods. It was hard to imagine technology without microchips.

Chuck told me that one of the pilots who flew a plane like this had been awarded the Victoria Cross. The plane had been hit and all of the hydraulics shut down. This meant that the gunner in the back was trapped. As the plane was going down, the pilot, instead of parachuting out, climbed to the back of the plane to attempt to free his crew member. He was successful. The gunner lived, but the pilot died when the plane crashed.

I imagined the plane falling from the sky. Time stops. Space narrows. Flames flicker across the plane's green body. The pilot clambers back on his knees along the low cave of the plane. There is the fizz of the radio from somewhere behind him. The sound of guns and the engine whining like a dying fly. The pilot calls out to the trapped gunner, "I'm on my way. I'll get you out. Don't worry." At some point, flames engulf the pilot, like a sudden rainstorm, and he can't see the gunner. Then the scene suddenly disappears into silence and blackness. The pilot's thoughts become individual atoms sent out into air, the way everything disappears when a radio is turned off, the radio signals buzzing about the air with nothing to receive them, nowhere to go.

OK. So maybe I could understand why Chuck and Dr. Tycho were so fascinated by plane crashes. I did want to know more about this pilot, about how the gunner must have felt after the crash, and what he said at the ceremony when the dead pilot's family received the Victoria Cross. I wondered what kind of stories the other crew members told or what the people on the ground thought when they saw the plane fall.

There was something mesmerizing about imagining how a large chunk of metal such as a plane could actually fly. Then to think of this same large chunk of metal dropping from the sky.

Nearby was a modern jet. Silver, sleek, with a pointed nose. An American Air Force plane. I climbed the narrow stairs to the cockpit and looked in. This wasn't at all like the other planes. It was filled with dials, switches, and other shining, flashing, gleaming gadgetry.

Chuck Ambersoll climbed up after me and smiled like he knew something. "Have you ever flown in a plane before?"

Of course, I hadn't.

"It's a fantastic experience." Chuck said.

Then it hit me (like a saxophone case might hit a bully on a school bus). Maybe I didn't have to wait for a cyclone to take me out of Kansas. If Chuck was flying out to Alberta, maybe I could find a way to come with him. I'd just have to work out how I could get my mother's permission since I'd be away overnight. But there was no way. She'd never let me . . . Besides, she needed me to look after her and she wasn't well. "Is there any way that you . . . I mean, for the interview . . . I'd really love to . . ."

"Fly?" Chuck said. "Ah. Well, like I was saying, when I was just a bit older than you, I was taken up in a plane . . . but I don't think there's time today. I'm flying out to Alberta tonight."

"But would it be possible — is there room if I wanted . . . I mean, I was thinking . . ." I put my foot on the brakes and came to a complete stop. Then I started again. "Could I fly with you to Alberta?" I didn't know if this was a ridiculous idea or even possible, let alone if I'd actually go if Chuck said yes.

"You'd like to fly to Alberta — tonight?" Chuck looked down at Dr. Tycho on the hangar floor. I couldn't tell what they thought of the idea.

"It'd be a great experience to write about — for the paper," I said hopefully.

Chuck turned toward me, sitting in the cockpit of the plane. "It would be a great opportunity for you, that's true. And I don't mind the company. But it would mean staying overnight." He looked out across the hangar at the other planes. "If your parents give the OK, it's all right with me."

Yikes.

I'd got this far. Was I actually going to go through with it?

A little teacher guy in my head pulled out a flipchart and began making a presentation.

> "Ahem. I'd like to welcome you to Alex's head, etc. etc. As I see it, the situation is this:
>
> "Alex is a teenager and he slammed someone at school. Then he took off. He doesn't want to have to deal with the principal, let alone the kid he slammed.
>
> "He's just asked to go on a plane ride halfway across the country and the pilot has said, 'Yes.' He could be in the clouds above the school by tonight, plucked from a difficult situation.
>
> "Should he go? Do we even have to ask this question, class?"

But then I heard myself — in my mind — standing up at the back of the classroom where the little guy was talking, and asking, "What about my mom? What about school? How long would we be gone for?"

Right. "How long would we be gone for, Chuck?"

"We'd land back in Kensington tomorrow afternoon, if everything goes according to plan."

The little guy began to make a big checkmark on the flipchart, but then instead picked up the flipchart and hurled it out the window. He held both his thumbs up.

But what about my mom?

I'd ask Uncle Barnard. She was HIS brother's wife, after all. I was just the kid. Even though he was a few wingtips short of a squadron, he could look after her. He could take some responsibility. I'd done my part for a long time. He could take a turn.

It was my turn to do something eccentric.

My chance to hurtle through the air toward Oz.

"I'll go home and talk to my mom. I'll get her permission," I told Chuck.

"She can call me, but I'd need something in writing, too."

"Oh . . . yes . . . right."

The truth was that I wasn't going to tell my mother. There was no chance that she'd let me go. I wanted things to work out the way I wanted them to, for a change. I'd write something up on the computer and then forge her signature. And like I said before, what she didn't know couldn't hurt me.

I'd arrange the rest with Uncle Barnard. I was going to *tell* him, not ask him. If I told Uncle Barnard that I was going, he'd have to look after her. Right?

That is, assuming I could find him. He might not be home. Perhaps he launched paper airplanes at highly secret locations, concealed behind stationery stores throughout the city.

After Chuck and I got down from the plane, Dr. Tycho came over and gave me a few aerial maps of Kensington.

"Thought you might like these. Yah?"

School was out by now, so I could go home. I'd have enough time to grab some clothes, write the letter, set some things up for Uncle Barnard, and then head over to his place to tell him the good news. I'd meet Chuck at the airport beside the museum by seven, and then we'd be Alberta bound.

eighteen

Alex Unbound

The first thing that I did when I got home was check my e-mail.

Nothing.

Well, nothing except a note about a rare Charlie Parker recording from this jazz **listserv** that I subscribed to. I was about to disconnect but I thought I'd check my e-mail one more time.

A message from bounce@bounce.net!

From: bounce@bounce.net
To: alexisaacson@hotmail.com
Subject: Re: Bouncing

I was bounce to run and now I'm bounce free. Charlie

Chaplin was the Little Tramp, I'm the tramponline.

The pebble doesn't rebound far from the stone.

And to think I'd asked for an explanation in my last message! The bad bounce puns were multiplying with, um, boundless energy. Maybe these messages were just a bunch of bad jokes, a kind of prank. Like those phone calls kids make:

Is Mr. Wall there? No, the person would answer.

Is Mrs. Wall there? No.

And now here comes the big yuk:

Are any of the walls there? No.

Then what's holding up the roof?

But I had the feeling that there was more to these messages than that. The last line of this message, about the pebble, didn't sound like a joke or a setup. The messages were probably a kind of code. I'd have to think awhile in order to solve them. Or else get an upgrade on my brain from the Wizard.

I opened up my word processor and wrote the note giving me permission to go out to Alberta with Chuck. After it was printed out, I signed my own name carefully. Well, almost my own name: "Marcia Firestone-Isaacson." I carefully folded the note and put it in an envelope.

There was some time left before I had to leave for Uncle Barnard's. I got out some paper and tried to solve the bounce.net message like an equation.

Perhaps the really bad puns actually meant something. "Bounce to Run" sounded like the old song "Born to Run," so:

Bounce to Run = Born to Run (an old song)

So then, if "Bounce" = "Born":

Bounce Free = Born Free.

I thought that was a song, too, so I looked it up on the Net. "Born Free" was an old book, movie, *and* song.

The next sentence was different. I wrote down what I thought it might be:

Tramponline = Tramp online and/or trampoline (more bouncing!)? The messages did come from the "bounce.net" domain.

The final sentence seemed like something different again:

The pebble . . . the stone = some kind of saying about part of a thing behaving like that thing, like children being a lot like their parents. What's the saying? The apple doesn't fall far from the tree.

I looked over what I had written down. "That was helpful!" I said out loud. I still had no idea what the message meant. I stuck the paper in my pants pocket. It was time to get going, and I needed to pack some underwear and things. Maybe Dorothy could travel for months in Oz without a toothbrush or a change of clothes, but I was certain that without these things, by morning my breath alone would be enough to stun a munchkin.

"The sun is bright today, but I can feel the stars hidden in the blue sky. They're telling me that your family needs you." My mom was working. I went into the kitchen to make us a quick supper. Baked beans and toast. Reheated macaroni and cheese. A few hotdogs. Now let me see. What wine goes with that?

I made a cup of instant coffee for my mom, opened a can of pop for me.

She'd finished the call by the time I came into her bedroom. I was carrying the tray of food that I'd made. I'd slaved all day over a hot microwave — for five minutes. I had returned later than usual and my mom was hungry. She'd long since eaten up all the food that I'd left out for her.

We ate without talking. Thankfully the phone didn't ring. It was nice to sit with her in the quiet and eat. It seemed especially silent, especially nice since I was about to leave, if only for one night. And she didn't say anything about the school having phoned her.

I helped her with her bedpan and then laid out some snacks beside her bed. I left her some water and her pills. I'd write Uncle Barnard a note about how to look after her while I took the bus over to his apartment.

I stuffed everything I needed into my backpack and told my mom that I was on my way to the library to finish a project for school. She kissed me on the forehead, and I was out the door.

nineteen

Saying Uncle

I didn't have any trouble finding my uncle's apartment. If I'd been blindfolded, spun around ten times, stuck in a deep-sea diving suit, locked in a crate with a clothespin clipped onto my nose, and *then* deposited in Uncle Barnard's building, I'd still have been able to follow my nose right to his door. His doorknocker (the perch) was fragrant, to say the least. I winced as I approached the door.

I could have used that clothespin.

I curled my hand into a fist and prepared to knock.

"HELLO! Nice to see you. Want some tea, sardines, an orange? Seen my frog painting?" Uncle Barnard had flung open the door just as I'd got into knocking range and began talking immediately. I considered throwing the note and running, but I had to make sure that he understood and that he'd actually look after my mother. Also, as soon as he'd opened the door, he began walking back down the hall into his apartment.

"Uncle Barnard — " I began.

"Apple dumplings," he interrupted. "You need them." He began clattering around in his kitchen, waving his arms about.

"I need you to do something, Uncle Barnard."

"Tea? You need tea?" He began patting his pockets furiously. "Tea?"

"No. I'm going away tonight. I need you to look after my mother." He turned toward me, his face serious, his arms frozen mid-rotation.

"Going . . . away?" A long pause. "Are you . . . coming back?"

"Yes, tomorrow. I just need you to look after Mom tonight and tomorrow during the day. I'll be back tomorrow night."

One of his hands started moving slowly back and forth. "Your mother?"

"She still can't get out of bed. I need you to help her. With food and whatever else she needs. I've made a list." I unfolded the note in my pants pocket and gave it to him.

"Bounce to run? Bounce free?" His face darkened. His eyes darted back and forth.

I'd given him the wrong note.

"What is this bounce? Where did you get this? What do you . . . ?"

"It's nothing. I gave you the wrong paper, Uncle." I pulled my notes about the bouncing e-mail out of his hands and passed him the list of things my mother needed. He didn't move his hands and the paper fluttered to the floor.

"It's nothing to worry about. It's just about something someone sent me."

"Who? Who sent you this? I . . . " He was rocking on his feet. It looked like he might either grab me or run away.

"It's nothing, Uncle. Just a note from a friend. Really. It's OK."

"A friend? This is a friend?" Uncle Barnard was panting.

"It's nothing. I just need you to help with my mother tonight." I picked up the list and handed it to him again. I didn't know why he was so upset. But, gradually, he became calmer, still making loud breathing sounds, but more slowly. He still seemed like he was trying to go two directions at once.

I told him to tell my mother that I was staying over at a friend's. That I'd be back the next day. That she shouldn't worry. He seemed to understand. We sat down at the little table outside the kitchen, and Uncle Barnard read the list carefully.

"You are coming back tomorrow."

"Yes."

"You are not leaving."

"No. I'll be back tomorrow."

He sat still for a few minutes.

"Uncle?"

"Tomorrow?"

"Yes."

"OK. I'll do it. I will help."

"Please remember to tell my mother not to worry." It was the first time I'd ever been away. I felt like a moon leaving its planet's orbit. Or, rather, a spaceship leaving earth. I had my own worries, but I didn't want those on the ground — my mother — to panic. We'd have to sort things out when I returned.

I left Uncle Barnard rummaging through piles of books, clothes, and other assorted objects in his living room, dredging up something from underneath a stack, then flinging it into a battered old suitcase.

As I walked down the dingy corridor leading from my uncle's, I wondered what my mother would say when he let himself into the house and appeared at the threshold to her room, one arm carrying the suitcase, the other spinning in the air, his mouth flapping furiously: "Alex has gone away. He told me to . . ."

twenty

Take Off, Eh?

It was only while riding the bus to the airport that it occurred to me: maybe Uncle Barnard had reacted so strongly when I gave him the wrong paper because he knew something.

What could Uncle Barnard know? Was "bouncing" some code that he understood? Judging from the books in his apartment, he certainly was into some pretty obscure things. But why would it be so upsetting? It wasn't just because he was so odd.

I'd talk to him when I returned.

Chuck was waiting for me at the main entrance. I gave him the note from my mother. He read it carefully, and, thankfully, didn't question my mother's signature. "OK, this is fine, but doesn't she want to speak to me?"

"No!" I said a bit too quickly. "I mean, my mother said if Clare arranged it, that is, if it's for the interview for Clare, then it's fine with her."

"All right, then. But I think I should speak with her anyway."

"You can't. I mean, she's at work now. She's hard to reach."

"Your father . . . ?"

"He's out of the picture."

"I see." Chuck put the letter in his pocket. "Your mother must place a lot of trust in you."

What did they call this in English class, dramatic irony? "Yes. Yes she does," I said.

"Well, just make sure to call her when we get to Alberta. In case she's worried. I'm sure it's not every day her kid flies halfway across the country."

Chuck led me briskly through the mostly empty airport and through a door marked Private Crew Only. From there we walked down a corridor and out a door onto the runway where there were about a dozen planes parked. A very large plane with FedEx painted on it was turning slowly into position. It was huge, like a whale on wheels, but its many lights were tiny like the eyes of a bug. It lumbered to a stop, and then, like ants around a fallen candy, airport attendants swarmed it — some wheeling the ladder up to the door, some at the various cargo bays, some in small strange vehicles, which attached different kinds of hoses to the plane. High above the tarmac, I could see the pilot in the cockpit taking notes and talking on his headset.

Chuck's plane — a two-seater — was waiting for us, pointing toward the runway. A man in blue coveralls told

Chuck that everything was ready. We climbed up the steps and crouched into the front of the plane. Chuck pointed to a seat and I sat down. Chuck quickly strapped himself in and then showed me how to pull the seatbelt over my head and fasten it over my chest. He passed me a headset to put on. It was like the ear protection someone using a jackhammer would use, except with a little microphone positioned in front of the mouth. The headset muffled much of the noise of the plane.

Chuck began speaking to the control tower. I could hear him over the headset. It sounded like someone was trying to push Rice Krispies though the radio. Even if I could have made out all of what they were saying, I would have had no idea what it meant.

"What's the ATIS?" Chuck asked. "OK, I have the echo on 134.25." Chuck was flicking various switches and checking things on the control panel.

"Kensington Tower, this is Golf Foxtrot Delta Hotel ready for take-off on runway 26." More Rice Krispies and we began moving down the runway. The plane rattled as the ground sped by us, and the engines were like enormous turbo-charged bees.

As soon as we were into the sky, everything changed. It was like plunging underwater. Everything moved more slowly and at the same time became clearer. Up in the sky, it was like the perfect sunny day — squared. The sky was bluer, the sun brighter. Some cosmic squeegee kid had cleaned off the windows of the world. We were on our way to Alberta. We'd be up in the sky for several hours. Now I'd know what it'd be like to be a migrating goose.

"So who is this Copper guy?" I'd been so excited to

escape out of the city that I hadn't asked any of the obvious questions.

"Dr. Tycho was talking to one of the pilots from out of town who is here for the aeronautical meeting — and he mentioned the crash, and the rumor that maybe this Nicholas Copper knew something. The pilot had heard that he'd moved out west but didn't know where. He did know someone in Copper's family — his sister, I think — who lived in Philadelphia and so we contacted her. She said that he was a bit of a recluse and plenty ornery. He lives in a farmhouse on a piece of land outside of a little town called One Hill, Alberta. And that's where we're headed."

The sun was sinking. Its slanting rays made everything golden. Mood lighting for heaven.

Or for a gloopy love story.

Or for those stories my mother told me about when my dad still lived at home.

What would my mother think if she were up here? Would she feel the closeness of the stars? They felt like prickles on the back of my neck. I closed my eyes and imagined my mother lifted off her bed, up above the clouds. Maybe she'd think the stars would have even greater control over your life when you were in the sky, in their world? You couldn't escape them up here.

One thing was for certain, though. My mother would be extremely angry with me for taking off without telling her and for lying about where I was going. Not that she could do anything about it. But perhaps I could dull her anger by talking about being close to the stars, so close that I could feel their breath.

It'd be worth a try. I wouldn't be able to just slam the door and sulk in my room like a normal teenager. I'd have to keep looking after her even though we were fighting. It's hard to keep up a good fight when you have to change the bedpan of the person you're fighting with.

Unless, of course, the arrangement with Uncle Barnard worked out permanently.

Nah.

That was even more unrealistic than imagining the stars breathing on me. But a guy could wish upon a panting star, couldn't he?

I loved flying in the plane, above the roads and fields, over the lakes and rivers. Chuck let me know which towns and cities we were above. We flew over Lake Huron, over part of Michigan, and then over Lake Superior. The land passed underneath us like a moving map, a vast video game.

Every ten or twenty minutes, Chuck would receive Rice Krispie contact from the radio. Mostly it was information about the weather. In between, Chuck told me stories about flying in the Air Force. Then he began to tell me a story about a famous plane crash.

The plane was a big jet carrying over 200 people. The engine on the tail exploded and shrapnel covered the body of the plane, severing all its hydraulics. This meant that the pilots couldn't control any of the flaps — there was nothing to stop the plane from flipping over, or nose-diving, and nothing to slow it down on landing, if it even made it that far. There was no procedure for this situation, since there was supposed to be no possibility that this could happen. It was like flying a paper airplane in a hurricane. The pilots were able to crash-land by flicking switches controlling the two remaining engines, crashing onto the runway, severing the cockpit, but saving 150 of the passengers and all but one of the crew. It was a miraculous landing.

Until Chuck told me this story, I hadn't thought that anything could go wrong on this flight. Flying seemed so natural and Chuck was so at ease. I must have begun to look worried, though. After all, it was my first flight. Chuck tried to reassure me.

"You know, Alex, statistics show you'd have to fly every day for 35,000 years to be assured of being in an accident. Even then, odds are you'd survive."

It was supposed to make me feel better, but I remembered the story of some airplane flying high above a city, emptying its toilets. The stuff froze as it dropped from the sky. A block of frozen pee hit a house, punching a hole in the roof. So what did the statistics say about that?

I didn't ask.

More Rice Krispies from the radio.

Chuck said something about our position into the microphone and said, "Alex, I study crashes. I research them. I want to know everything about them. I believe that I can learn from them. And then I can help prevent them. My parafoils are a step toward this. Yet some crashes are a riddle, a puzzle, a mystery . . ."

"Like the one the man in Alberta knows about."

"Bingo."

twenty-one

Someone Else's Troubles

"We're getting ready to land." It was the middle of the night. I'd fallen asleep and was woken by Chuck's voice. The ground was a black sky without moon or stars. And there were no lights anywhere except for a few dim lines on the horizon in front of us. "I've made arrangements for the landing strip to stay open. It requires just one person — really all he needs to do is to flick off the lights when we're done. You don't need much, way out here."

Chuck pointed the plane at the ground and in a few moments, and lots of shaking, we touched down and were driving along the runway, still shaking. Truth be told, so was I.

"Don't worry," Chuck said. "We won't fall apart. You

know what they say about planes: twelve-thousand parts all flying in close formation."

Near the end of the runway, there was a small building. An old guy walked out to meet us. He must have been the Chief Illumination Technologist, since he would be the one to turn off the lights. Chuck handed him a rolled-up hundred-dollar bill. "Thanks."

There was a beaten-up old car waiting for us. When we closed the trunk, we could see our luggage through the rust holes. Chuck seemed to have thought of everything. I guess he was used to planning "missions." It's not much good knowing where to jump if you've forgotten the parachutes.

We could also see the ground rushing past us through the floor as we started down the gravel road.

It was half an hour in the opposite direction from One Hill to get to the nearest motel where Chuck had reserved a room. The Wheat Horse Inn and Tavern ("Good Drinks, Fine Food, Rooms"). It wasn't any newer than the car, but at least you couldn't see the ground through its floors. What we could see, through the glass door, were ancient red carpets riddled with cigarette burns. Chuck rang the bell and a bent-over old man with greased-back hair emerged from behind the bar (he must have had a fold-up bed back there). He let us in and Chuck signed the registration book at the bar.

"No drinking in the room," the man said. "Breakfast at seven. Harrrgh." He paused to hawk behind the bar. "The key."

It was attached to a huge piece of wood that looked like it had been broken off a banister.

No chance that we could accidentally walk away with it in our pockets.

Unless it got mixed up with the golf clubs in there.

Or my wooden leg.

"Checkout at eleven," the man said. "What brings you two fellers out here?"

"We got business with a guy called Nicholas Copper over in One Hill. You heard of him?"

"You want to be careful with that guy. If I were a chicken, I'd watch my eggs, you know what I mean?"

Chuck grinned. "I can take care of myself."

"Well, watch the kid. Around here, there ain't a face that one Saturday night or another hasn't made the acquaintance of Nicholas Copper's fist." The man slipped behind the bar and disappeared.

Our room had a door that looked as if someone had made a hobby of kicking it. Two frail, sad, little beds were draped in mustard-colored blankets and yellowing sheets. Chuck saw my expression. "We'll only be here for a few hours.

"Besides, all the rooms at the Ritz were taken . . . for the Russian royal family reunion."

Considering how much had happened that day — from the incident on the bus to ending up in a hotel room in One Hill, Alberta — it was no wonder that as soon as I was near the bed, I surrendered to its gravitational pull. I flopped down and fell asleep almost immediately. I was too tired to dream about anything, not about the blonde-haired woman floating around my house, nor of my possible stint in a prison orchestra, playing with other musicians who'd used their cases as weapons.

It was only a few hours later when Chuck woke me. The view outside was pearly gray. "You learn to get up early when you've been in a war," Chuck said with too much energy for that time of the morning.

They made us greasy eggs and coffee down at the bar. No chance of Sugar Blam! cereal for me here. We were the only ones there except for the old guy and a woman in a stained white apron who acted as cook and waitress and who could have been the old guy's sister. Or mother. You couldn't tell. There was also a man who had the standard-issue stocky build of a trucker, sucking back coffee and an enormous plate of eggs.

Back in Ontario it would be light out, so I decided to phone my mother. I was worried about her. Not to mention about how Uncle Barnard was doing.

But I didn't want her to get worked up, or lecture me, so I dialed the number for Starbright. I would disguise my voice.

I entered my mother's credit card number when the recording asked me to. I'd have to explain this later, though she rarely looked at the bills. Paying bills was my job.

"Starbright," my mother said. "I'm here to listen for you."

"Yes, I'm, I mean, I've got a . . . predicament." I tried to speak in my lowest voice, covering half of the receiver with my hand, the way people in movies do.

"Maybe I can help. Maybe I can help you with your predicament." She sounded so earnest and helpful. I felt like I really could tell her all my troubles.

But I remembered that my troubles were the troubles of a low-voiced man.

"It's just that I . . ." I thought of the trucker in the bar. "I'm away from my family, driving a truck. And my wife . . ." I paused to think of what problems I was having with my wife.

"You're feeling lonely. You miss your wife and children . . ."

"Yes, I mean, I'm on the road a lot and . . . when I'm away I think about . . . There are things I don't know. Things that I want to know." It was harder than I expected, having someone else's troubles.

"You want answers, of course. I'm trying to hear what the stars are saying about this. I think you have questions not only when you're on the road."

"Yes."

"They're family questions."

I lost my nerve and hung up.

Chuck was waiting in the hall. "Ready for 'departure?'"

twenty-two

Copper Mine

"His name is Nicholas Copper. He used to build and fly experimental aircraft out of a little hangar in Kensington." The old car crackled and bumped over the gravel road that led toward One Hill. It was just after 6:30 in the morning and our breaths made clouds as we spoke in the cold car (the heater, of course, was broken). Chuck was filling me in. "The plane flown by the girl was experimental — it was supposedly built by her father, which is why it's very likely that Copper knows something. Copper flew out of Kensington at that time, about twelve or so years ago."

Chuck explained that, as far as he and Dr. Tycho had been able to find out, the girl, her father, and the other man didn't actually fly out of the Kensington airport, but there were some airplane enthusiasts in the city who knew something about them. They'd occasionally caught a glimpse of their odd-looking aircraft flying over the city. The whole thing sounded a bit like an urban legend, a flying Loch Ness Monster story.

"They were trying to fly across Canada?" I asked. It seemed unlikely that a homemade airplane could do this.

"That's what the story is."

"And the girl was ten?"

"It seems like she was probably about that."

"How could she possibly fly a plane at that age?"

"Some kids learn that young. And it wasn't a solo flight — she had two adults flying with her. But you're right — she was hardly old enough, especially for a home-built plane. Who knows how it flew? The whole thing was crazy. We've heard that they took off in terrible weather, too. Bad idea. What kind of crankshaft of a father she had, I don't know . . ."

For the next while, I sat back in the big vinyl seat as we drove, only half awake.

"So tell me," Chuck asked after some time, "what'd you do to be assigned 'an unscheduled holiday' from school?"

"What?" I rather quickly became more awake.

"Why were you invited to explore some other educational options for a while?"

"Other options . . . ?" I still wasn't completely awake.

"Why were you suspended?"

"Oh." I finally clued in. "I wasn't. I just took off because I hit a guy on the school bus."

"What'd he do? Was it about a girl?"

Back at home, kids would be walking to school. Others would be running for the bus, their mouths filled with toast. E-mails were probably being sent to my server, waiting there like idling cars outside a convenience store. Uncle Barnard would be extracting teabags from his pockets, making lint tea for my mother. "It's good. It's from a good shirt. I've had it for years," he'd be saying, his arms scrambling the air. My mother would be wrinkling her forehead, looking doubtful, worrying about me.

Was it about a girl?

I hoped Annie was also wondering about where I'd got to and what I was doing. I was sure she wasn't imagining that I was in a rust-pocked car trundling down a gravel road on the way to One Hill, Alberta, in the early morning.

"No," I said. "It wasn't about a girl. It was just some jerk insulting my mother."

"So you hit him?"

"Yes."

"Can't argue with that. Might have done the same myself. What'd the teachers say?"

"I don't know. I haven't been back."

At school, the principal would be walking into his office. He'd pour himself a cup of coffee and set it down on his desk, in front of the framed photograph of his family. Then he would pick up the telephone, dial the number to my house, and speak with my mom. "Yesterday morning, there was an altercation on the school bus. Your son, Alex, was responsible . . ."

For some reason, it seemed he hadn't called yesterday. And if he hadn't, then he'd be sure to call today.

"It's not for me to tell you what to do," Chuck said.

"But the way I figure it, you gotta take things like a man. Don't go AWOL. Sure, deck the guy, but then own up to it and face the consequences."

Consequences.

Matt was likely prowling my neighborhood, scowling, punching his fist into his cupped left hand, his head bandaged and his eyes narrowed, scanning the streets for me.

"There'll be plenty of consequences once I go home. For now though, I'm not gonna worry about it."

Chuck asked me to open his briefcase and take out a file labeled "Kensington Experimental Plane Crash: Alberta." In the file were some directions from One Hill to Nicholas Copper's farm and a map. We were to take County Road 15 north until Miller's Sideroad. We'd go west for about five miles and then there'd be a dirt road running south. At the end of this road would be Copper's farmhouse. It'd take a couple hours to get there from One Hill.

Of course, we missed the dirt road the first time and had to double back after a few miles. Practically everywhere around us was flat, except for the dirt road. It ran along what might have been a dried-out streambed and across a little ravine.

We might have damaged some of the rust on the borrowed car. The structural rust.

Nicholas Copper's farmhouse was rundown yet immaculate. The paint was peeling from the windows and half the shingles on the roof were gone. But there was nothing out of place in the little yard — not a weed, not an overturned barrel, not a tire or rusted tractor. It was strangely empty. If I'd been told that Nicholas Copper vacuumed his yard once a day, I'd have believed it.

Chuck opened his door with a creak. He waited for me to open mine and climb out of the car. Then he strode up to the wooden front door and knocked.

"Mr. Copper?" he said.

Nothing.

I thought to myself: We've flown halfway across the country and he's out doing groceries or buying vacuum-cleaner supplies.

There was some movement in the window.

"Mr. Copper?"

The window opened a few inches. A dark stick was pushed out of it. It took me a few seconds to realize that it was the barrel of a gun. Chuck motioned to me to move back behind the car.

I slid behind the car's wide trunk then lowered myself to bumper level. I could hardly breathe. It was a movie where I was suddenly pulled out of the audience and stuck on screen for the shoot-out scene. And not being able to see what was happening made it much worse.

"I'm a pilot, Mr. Copper. I'm just here to talk . . . Your sister thought we'd have a lot in common. Your sister in Philadelphia." Chuck spoke slowly and very calmly. He'd probably talked a few crazy soldiers out of blowing themselves and their platoons back to mama. Chuck held his hands in front of his chest, palms out.

I heard the click of the gun being cocked.

What would I do if he shot Chuck?

I looked around to see where I could run.

"I'm a friend of Dr. Tycho's. From Kensington. I'm just here to talk. I'm . . . not the police." Chuck spoke in his mellowest, most reasonable voice.

"What you called?" The voice was tight and rough. The kind of voice Rumplestiltskin would have had.

"Chuck Ambersoll. And the boy here is a young friend of mine — Alex."

Nothing. The gun remained motionless in the window.

"Look, we're not . . . the authorities. If we were, we wouldn't be driving such a heap of a car, and I wouldn't have brought the kid with me. We're just here to talk."

A pause and then the gun was drawn back into the window.

A gaunt, stooped-over man with sideburns and a leather vest appeared at the door. He was probably around fifty. "Come in," he drawled. "Never can be too sure."

twenty-three

Raising Dust

"Seen things I didn't want ta. Was places I shouldn'ta been. Always on the watch for lawmen." Nicholas Copper snapped open a can of beer and sucked in the foam that bubbled onto the top. He pulled a chair out from under a battered kitchen table and sat down. He didn't offer us anything to drink. He didn't offer us a seat. "Come all the way out here. Think I know anything?"

Chuck dragged a chair — slowly — from under the table and sat down. Then paused. Now that there was no gun, he wasn't letting anyone else, ah . . . call the shots. I tentatively pulled a chair a few inches out from under the table and sat on the edge of it.

"Listen," he began. "My buddy Tycho tells me you flew out of the Kensington Airstrip about ten years ago."

"Many did."

"Experimental aircraft."

"OK."

"So perhaps you know something about that home-built that went down with the little girl in it."

Copper had the beer can tipped to his lips, but froze mid-swig, then put it down on the table.

"Don't know about that."

"Look," Chuck said. "I'm not a cop. I'm a flyer, an inventor like yourself. I heard people saying things about this crash. I'm just curious about what happened is all."

"That's mighty curious, coming out here. What's the kid for?"

"He's just along for the flight. A field trip."

Copper looked at me across the table, his head tilted cynically. He wasn't buying it.

I took a chance. "I bashed someone at school. I'm laying low." "Laying low" — it still sounded like it was from a bad TV western, except this time, it was a rerun.

"Haw!" Copper grunted suddenly, laughing. "Those were the days. Haw! I like this kid. I've bashed a few myself. Lemme get you guys beer. Bashed someone, haw!"

He got two silver cans out of the fridge, opened them both with a snap, and plunked them down on the table so that the foam came out.

"Thanks," Chuck said, making a "cheers" motion with the beer can, then drinking.

"Thanks," I said to Copper, and made a "cheers" motion just like Chuck's. I was back to being the deep-voiced trucker who had called Starbright.

I took a few sips of the beer. I didn't want to offend

Copper. He seemed to like that I was a tough kid.

Sure, I was tough.

Tough like Toto.

Copper tipped his chair back on two legs. "OK. So there was a guy back in Kensington, definite strange one. Made crackpot home-builts. Real weird stuff — one in the shape of a frog. Was a wonder they could move, let alone get into the air. Got it into his head to fly across the country. The Frog in the Sky Tour. Something like that."

Flying frogs! This was beginning to sound familiar.

"Do you recall his name?" Chuck asked.

I had a feeling I knew what the name was going to be.

"Barnard," I hissed under my breath, hoping I was wrong.

"Barnard — yes, that's the man. Barnard Isaacson."

As Chuck had said to me earlier, "Bingo!" I had the horrified feeling that the stars were setting this all up. Some kind of cosmic practical joke, setting up a bunch of coincidences for me to trip over.

Chuck looked at me, wondering what was going on.

I didn't know either, but I wasn't going to let on quite yet, and certainly not in front of Nicholas Copper. I'd learned about keeping my cards to my chest playing poker with my mother.

"You and Dr. Tycho were talking about him earlier."

"Right," Chuck said. "Dr. Tycho mentioned him." Chuck looked at me for an uncomfortably long time then turned back to Copper.

"Know this guy?" Copper asked.

"No, Tycho just knew the name. We didn't know this Barnard Isaacson was involved."

"Most didn't. Kept to himself. Just him and a friend."

Copper drained his beer. "And a kid. They wanted the kid to fly the plane."

"Across the country?"

"The three of them."

Copper didn't know the name of the other guy. And he didn't know who the kid was.

It didn't surprise me to hear that Barnard was the crazy builder of the frogplane, though I'd thought that he'd become crazy only after whatever it was that sent my mother to bed. He had worked in an ad agency, after all.

I thought of the note that I'd found in Uncle Barnard's book. *We can do it. She'll be ready soon.*

"She" could mean either the plane or the kid. And what did my father have to do with all of this?

Nicholas Copper went to the door, still with a beer in his hand. "Walk," he said.

So we walked. Chuck and I left our beers on the table. Copper took us along a scraggy path beside a scraggy field at the back of his house. The field seemed to be for raising dust, and the crop was doing well. The sky was all around us, and it was an empty blue like the TV screen before a video starts. We walked in silence. There was only the occasional sound of Copper sucking beer out of the can. And belching. I thought of science class — "for every action an equal reaction."

"Where were you when this Barnard fellow was building the frogplane?" Chuck finally asked.

"You sound like a cop." Copper stopped walking.

"I mean, how do you know about this? Did you ever talk to him?"

"I don't like no cops," Copper said. "I don't know anything."

Pause. Copper looked as thoughtful as I imagined he ever looked. Then he belched — contemplatively, I think.

"I talked to him. Tried to talk him out of flying with the girl. He was half-cracked, like I said. His plane was a sorry piece of junk. Tried to help him by . . . no, never mind." He started walking quickly.

Chuck looked over at me. A "we have something here" kind of look.

"Mr. Copper, I only want to know about the actual flyers. If you helped him with the plane, I'd be interested to know what you saw. I won't compromise your privacy. Anything you tell me about your involvement will remain with me. I collect the stories of these crashes for my own interest. There'll be no report or anything. And Alex won't say anything, right?"

"Of course not."

As we walked around the dust field, Copper told us that he'd helped Uncle Barnard with some of the building of his plane. When Uncle Barnard ran into a snag, he called Copper, who'd done some work repairing planes for the Air Force. Because of his involvement, Copper was worried that he might be somehow held responsible for the plane crash.

Responsible because the girl had died.

"She actually died?" I said.

"And there was no investigation? No inquest?" Chuck asked, amazed. "How could a girl be killed and no explanation be given, no parents heard from, no trace in the papers. I know that there was talk about a kid's death, but I've found no record . . ."

"I don't go around meddling in other people's affairs. I don't ask no questions." Copper sounded surly. He'd had enough questions.

It was shortly after the crash that Copper left Kensington and moved out to Alberta. "Like I said, seen things I didn't want ta. Was places I shouldn'ta been. And not just that crash." He looked at us meaningfully.

I was sure he was going to belch. But instead he seemed to hear the refrigerator call his name — by this time we had returned to his empty backyard. He went inside to get himself another beer. It was as if, unlike the Wicked Witch of the West, he needed to souse himself, or else he'd melt away.

"Do you believe him, Alex?" Chuck asked as we waited outside.

It hadn't occurred to me that he might have been lying.

"It could have been him in that plane. He might know more information about the girl and why there was no investigation. He might know more about this Barnard Isaacson. People often know more than they let on." It was his turn to look at me meaningfully, and there was no sign of a burp in sight.

Did he know that I'd lied about knowing Uncle Barnard?

Nicholas Copper emerged again. "Don't talk to no one. Don't ask questions. Don't tell no one nothing. I still have friends."

It sounded like a threat. Any friends of Copper's weren't the kind you'd meet at the ballet.

"Of course not, Mr. Copper. I greatly appreciate your

candor. You have my assurance that everything you have told us will be kept in the strictest confidence," Chuck said as if reading from a letter.

"Except for what I tell Dr. Tycho, and anyone else who wants to know," Chuck added once we'd closed the car doors and started off down the dry trail from Copper's farm.

twenty-four

Sledgehammer

We headed back toward One Hill through the flat blond wheat fields. If we didn't get lost, we'd get back in a couple of hours, around lunchtime. We would stop for a bite and then drive to the airstrip. I was looking forward to flying in daylight, to watching the ground unfold like a huge movie beneath us. And, armed with my big-time reporter's notebook, I'd be able to fill in a few more details about being a pilot for my interview with Chuck.

Cruising along the empty country roads, Chuck was tapping his thumbs on the steering wheel, nodding his head slightly.

I was thinking too. There seemed to be more and more people, more and more explanations that needed to be found. I was a teenager — wasn't I supposed to be skateboarding or something? It'd sure be easier if I could've relied on the stars to tell me everything I needed to know. But then again, being able to read stars certainly hadn't helped my mom deal with the world. I had to get answers, not from the sky.

From the ground.

If it had been Uncle Barnard who'd crashed the plane, he had some explaining to do. I was going to find out what happened. Maybe I'd take his frog painting hostage. That'd get him to talk.

First: This girl who'd died in the crash, who was she?

Second: Who was the other person in the frogplane?

Third: (This space reserved for Alex to panic.)

Fourth: Did my father have anything to do with the crash?

Fifth: If Copper knew Barnard, then he'd have known my father. Or else . . . he was my father . . .

No.

That'd really be too much like a TV movie. Besides, Copper had a sister in Philadelphia, and I'd never heard about an aunt. But why wouldn't my mother just tell me that my father was dead, if he was? Or why wouldn't she tell me if he'd become a recluse in Alberta? Even if he was one like Nicholas Copper?

I had that itchy e-mail feeling again, the one where I wanted to make contact. How did the settlers heading West manage to leave everything behind? How did my father?

Finally, we pulled into One Hill, which also had One Street and One Restaurant, the Daisy Q Diner. While Chuck went into the restaurant, I stopped at the One Payphone. I wanted to check on my mother. I thought of the scene in the *Wizard of Oz* where Dorothy has run away and gets the huckster from Omaha to look in his crystal ball and tell her how Auntie Em is doing, like some kind of live Webcam site. If only Dorothy had had Uncle Henry's credit card.

"Starbright here. I can listen to the stars for you." She sounded tired, less confident than usual.

I made my voice breathy and said the first thing that came into my head: "I am far away. I need to know about my father."

"Even when it is daytime, the stars shine. You just have to look for them."

This could have been about anything or anybody. No-name psychic advice. One sign fits all.

"Where do I look for my father?"

"Like a bird, your father has flown away."

"My father flew? In an airplane? Did it crash?"

A gasp and then silence. She was holding her breath. What could she have seen in the stars?

"Hello?"

"The stars say . . . the stars say that . . . I can feel . . . if you were meant to find your father . . . many people live without their father. You are far away — you are . . . where?"

I hung up the phone. I didn't know if she knew it was me. I guessed I'd find out when I returned home to face the music.

I didn't expect it to be very tuneful.

Inside the Daisy Q, Chuck was sitting in a two-seater booth at the back. The teak-colored wood of the booth was covered in graffiti, some scratched into the wood, some written in black marker. Beside Chuck's right ear it said,

"Vernon loves Bonnie" inside a big heart. But instead of an arrow through the heart, there was a hammer. I had no idea what that meant — loving Bonnie is like having your heart slammed by a sledgehammer? Vernon made Bonnie's heart beat as powerfully as a hammer? Cupid was actually a house framer?

"We have a problem." Chuck looked grim. "Someone smashed up my plane. The old guy who was at the landing strip was just on the phone with the owner over there." Chuck motioned at a man in a white apron standing behind the counter. "News travels fast in a small town. Apparently, the windshield is shattered and there are holes in the wings."

I thought of Vernon — the guy who loved Bonnie — taking his hammer to Chuck's plane. A crime of passion. I did it for you, Bonnie.

"So we're stuck in Alberta until I can either get the plane repaired or get someone to fly us out of here."

"Great!" I said sarcastically.

I had been glad not to have to deal with the school situation for a day, and, for that matter, to have a break from looking after my mom, but this was turning out to be much more complicated. I was becoming seriously AWOL. My mother would start to freak, if she hadn't already. And as for Uncle Barnard, every day I was away was another opportunity for him to wander off and forget about my mother. Or to try to cook a turkey in the furnace and burn the house down. Or to do some other crazy thing that I couldn't even imagine.

Soon, I was going to have to tell my mother where I was.

"I'm going to assess the damage and then drive to the

closest big town — Samson — to see about getting the plane repaired. Soon as we know what's going on, you should call home and let your mom know. Maybe I can get a buddy to fly out and take us back to Kensington. We'll leave right after lunch. OK?"

No. I was going to call one of *my* buddies to fly us home.

I didn't exactly have any other choices. Except seeing if I could be a guest at the charming and well-appointed guesthouse of your gracious host Nicholas Copper.

I'd rather live with coyotes.

I had a fantastic Western omelette before we left. If they couldn't make one out here, where could they?

The plane was a mess. It looked like a car wreck. There were holes punched into both wings, and the front windshield and one of the side windows were smashed. It looked like the propeller had tried to make a milkshake out of a mountain.

And lost.

"Why would anyone do this?" I asked.

"Never mind why," Chuck said. "Who?" Just the look in his eyes could have made a milkshake out of any mountain.

Especially if the mountain had anything to do with wrecking his plane.

"Do you think Nicholas Copper had something to do with it?" I remembered how threatening he'd sounded.

Chuck was looking down the runway, thinking. "Maybe," he finally said. "Maybe."

twenty-five

The Cosmic Joystick

The city of Samson was so small it could fit in the pocket of a wheat farmer and there'd still be room for the keys to the tractor. It was the biggest city in the region, yet it only had a population of about 30,000. On this day, 30,002. We arrived in the late afternoon. Chuck stopped at a gas station on the edge of town to make a few arrangements. Someone to drive down and bring his plane back to be fixed. A place to stay. A call to somewhere to try to get someone to fly us home. Chuck had told me that he expected it would take awhile to get his plane fixed, if anyone in Samson could do it at all. Parts would need to be ordered at the very least. You couldn't just buy parts for a plane in your local hardware store. ("Just over there, sir, in the aisle marked 'Worms, Nails, Airplane Parts.'")

Chuck left me downtown to look around while he made further arrangements about his plane. On the back of an envelope, he wrote out the directions and phone number to a bed-and-breakfast that he'd reserved for us. It'd be our communications center. We could stay in touch by leaving messages there if we needed to. And we'd meet there later.

It was kind of exciting, really, to be in the middle of even a small city, far away from home, with nothing to do but explore.

I'd begin by cataloguing the local butterfly species.

Right.

I started walking down Main Street, which, through some subtle feat of deduction, I took to be one of the main streets of Samson. There were department stores, CD shops, discount clothing stores, fast-food restaurants (of quite an exotic variety — they didn't have drive thrus!), and quite a few funky stores that sold . . . funky things: strange shoes, odd clothes, candleholders that looked either seven hundred years old or like they were from Mars, and furniture made out of plastic or twigs. Or both.

In the windows and plastered on telephone poles and walls were posters advertising concerts in bars. "Average Mean and the Belt Curves" were at Drummore's. "Baskethead" was at Fat Charlie's. "Big Plastic Flatfoot" was opening for "Henry Penny and the Sky Is Falling" at Matilda's. And that night at the Playhouse, Gord Thomas would be performing from his latest CD, *Fables from the Blizzard*.

"WHAT!?" I said out loud. "WHAT!?"

Just when I thought I was on my own, that I was

actually living my own story, here was another one of these star-driven coincidences: Gord Thomas.

As in "Annie" Thomas.

Annie's father was playing that night in Samson.

I could almost hear my mother saying, "I told you so."

But then I thought, these are my OWN unbelievable coincidences, not anyone else's, even if the stars seem to be working the joystick on the cosmic Nintendo.

So now I knew my plans for the evening. I wondered if Gord Thomas would be surprised that I knew his daughter.

It was getting dark so I walked to the hotel that Chuck had reserved for the night. Actually, I walked away from it, then perpendicular to it, until I was finally able to figure out the directions I'd been given. It was a bed-and-breakfast called Delilah's Inn. Cute, eh? We were in Samson, after all. I'd have bet that somewhere in the city there was a Samson's Hair Salon. Or maybe that would be Delilah's. Either way, who said the world didn't need more bad jokes?

Oh, yeah: Annie.

I introduced myself to the woman writing at a little desk behind a little counter. She smelled as if a truck carrying soap had crashed into a flower shop. "There should be a reservation for two under Ambersoll."

"Oh, yes, yes, dearie. There certainly is. The reservation was just made. Your father called us this afternoon."

What? My *father*?

Oh, yeah: Chuck. "Actually, Mr. Ambersoll isn't my father. We're just traveling together."

She looked like she was waiting for an explanation. I knew I didn't need to give one so I said, "a field trip."

As if that made it clearer.

"Oh, of course, dearie. A field trip. Well, isn't that lovely? A field trip."

"Which is our room?" I didn't want any more questions. Maybe she was the principal's sister. Or Matt's aunt. I hadn't checked the stars lately, so who knew?

The room was "lovely." Filled with antique furniture, with flowers all over it, and pictures of old black-and-white guys with curly beards and serious expressions. There were also pictures of women. They could have been their wives, mothers, or daughters. It was hard to tell, just like the woman at the hotel. They all had that serious expression that seemed to run in the family (maybe it was because they'd all had to use the same outhouse in winter). The sink was inside the room and had old-fashioned brass taps. On every available surface there were bowls of powerfully scented pink flower fragments, debris from the accident that had produced the receptionist lady's perfume. The telephone was black and it had a rotary dial. I'd never used a rotary dial. I could imagine Alexander Graham Bell using it. "Look, I've just invented the telephone, and I'm very hungry. I wonder if you could deliver a large pizza with everything? Sure . . . I'll hold . . ."

I'd have to use that funny rotary dial to phone my mother. Not Starbright my mother, but my mother mother. I'd have to dial our personal number, not the star-reading line, and really talk to her. I couldn't be gone another day without talking to her.

I took a deep breath.

With each number I dialed I had to wait forever for

the little dialing wheel to return to its starting place, but eventually I dialed the whole number.

The phone hadn't even finished its first ring when my mother picked it up. "Barnard, is that you? Where are you? Have you found Alex?"

I hung up.

I just couldn't talk to her.

I didn't want her to be worried, and I certainly didn't want Uncle Barnard out looking for me and not looking after my mother, but I couldn't really tell her that I'd hitched a plane ride out to Alberta, and now because the plane had been smashed, I was in a hotel room that smelled like the epicenter of an air-freshener disaster, and not to wait up. She'd sounded so upset when I'd called her on the Starbright line and asked about my father, about plane crashes.

I had to take charge. But did that mean I had to tell the truth?

I should tell the truth.

I'd been abducted by little green space aliens who wanted to introduce me to an advanced civilization based on shoelaces, the number three, and limes.

Arrgh.

Wait. I'd call Annie's mother. Maybe I could get her to check on my mother, to tell her that I was OK. I had already told her that my mom was confined to bed. I didn't want anyone to know about my mother, but out of everyone, she'd understand. Besides, there was nobody else.

Could I ask her to keep a secret from Annie?

I got Annie's number from directory assistance and dialed.

"Hello, is Clare there?"

"Alex? We've been worried about you. Is everything all right? Where are you?" It was Annie.

"I'm okay. I'm in, um, Alberta."

"Alberta! Now that's skipping school in style. Leaving town for the Wild West like an outlaw! What are you doing there and when are you coming back?"

I explained why I was in Alberta and what had happened to Chuck's plane.

"There are all sorts of rumors flying — whoops, no pun intended — around school about you. But no one would believe that you're actually in Alberta. There's been a bunch of kids who've told the principal about what Matt and Bud have done to them. You were the only one who actually stood up to them, though. Also, Mr. Wagner said that if you can't make it to practice, he may have to give our *Wizard of Oz* duet to someone else."

"Tell him I'll be back soon. Unless . . . have I been suspended?"

"I don't know. They have to talk to your parents first. Have you talked to your mom?"

"Sort of. Actually that's why I called. My mom's sick in bed. I thought that maybe your mom could help."

While her mom came to the phone, I told Annie that her dad was performing in town that night and that I was going. She thought that was very cool.

And weird.

Annie gave the phone to her mom. "Mom, it's Alex. He's going to hear Dad play. In Alberta!"

When she came on the line, I explained to Clare that I was with Chuck in Alberta, shadowing "the interviewee." Then I told her what had happened to Chuck's plane and about my mom's situation. Of course, she said she'd help. I knew she would.

I also told her about Uncle Barnard. "He's not all there," I said, "and right now he's not there at all, though he was supposed to be looking after my mom."

Clare said she'd go right over. Then later she'd make some meals to bring. She'd also tell my mom that she'd spoken to me. "But perhaps your mother would like it if you called yourself?" she suggested.

Of course, she would.

But I liked how Clare didn't pressure me.

"My mom . . . she's kind of . . . I don't want Annie to know about her condition."

Clare said she understood.

"And you tell Gord at the concert tonight that he should treat you nice. You tell him Annie and I said so," she laughed.

After I hung up I lay back on my pink-fringed bed with the fluffy pillow. I imagined Clare walking into my house. There'd be all my boots and shoes cluttering up the front hall. The bench piled with flyers that I hadn't recycled yet, and books and backpacks and plastic bags that I'd left. There'd be a trail of my laundry scattered across the floor. She'd hear my mother talking quietly on the phone, talking long distance with the stars. It'd be quite dark, my mom under the dim light of an old lamp. Clare would peer around the half-open door into my mother's room, unable to figure out what part of the large shape was my mom and what part was the bed. Then she'd realize how large my mother was and why she was stuck in bed. She'd nod her head knowingly. She'd look around the messy kitchen piled high with dirty dishes and half-eaten food, until my mother finished on the phone. "Hello, Mrs. Isaacson," Clare would say, quietly knocking on her bedroom door.

Then Uncle Barnard would blast through the front door, his arms wheeling about, clomping over the boots and shoes. "Alex is here?" he'd shout. "I looked in the river. I looked in the fire station. I looked in the gazebo. I looked in everywhere." And he'd plunge into my mother's bedroom holding a lint-covered teabag up above his head. "Marcia, it is time to make tea."

twenty-six

A Rolling Stone Gathers No Loss

I waited for a while for Chuck to return. He didn't and so I left a note on what was going to be Chuck's pink-fringed bed with the fluffy pillow. I didn't need to wait around. I didn't need Chuck's permission. He wasn't a parent or a teacher. This was *my* trip out of Kansas. I walked down the creaky staircase and nodded 'bye to the receptionist lady. She tilted her head, wondering what I was doing — as if going out was unusual. I almost said, "I'm off to Mesopotamia. Hold all my calls."

But I didn't.

I had a "dinner combo" at the Samson Burger down the street and read the CD reviews in the Samson College newspaper left on the table beside me. It was time to find the Playhouse and get ready to hear Gord Thomas.

The Playhouse. It sounded distinguished, as if it regularly had string quartet concerts, classical theater, and screenings of old French films.

But it wasn't.

It was a dumpy bar. There was even nude dancing advertised for the following Saturday night. The Playhouse was all shake and no speare. And they weren't going to let me in. I was underage. They wouldn't be asking for my ID at the door — they could tell my age a mile away at midnight. All my ID was good for was a student bus pass. But I hadn't come this close only to tell Annie that I'd missed her dad's concert.

I slipped into the alley beside the Playhouse. There was a bunch of wrappers and papers and the remains of some kind of human food, though I couldn't tell which. A cat, dining in style on the contents of a tipped-over garbage can, leaped onto a fence and ran away. It was the kind of alley where in the movies something bad would happen. But I figured this was Samson, not New York. How bad could it be?

They wouldn't ask for my ID around back. At least not on the other side of what looked to be a half-open bathroom window. I set straight the tipped-over trashcan, found its lid behind a decaying cardboard box, and covered over its smelly contents. Then I climbed on top of it and went feetfirst into the open window. I felt around with my feet for something to stand on and found what seemed to be the back of a toilet.

I lowered myself.

There was a clattering and then something shattered on the ground, fizzing.

It wasn't the back of a toilet.

I pulled the rest of me in and looked around.

Gord Thomas and his band looked back. I was standing in what was left of their supper, having just knocked over the first installment of their night's drinks.

Silence.

More silence.

Then still more silence punctuated with the sound of dripping liquids.

"Hi! I know your daughter," I finally said to Gord Thomas. I recognized him from his CDs at Annie's house.

Silence.

More silence.

I shifted uncomfortably.

Then Gord started giggling.

After a second, the rest of the band came in with an accompaniment of snorting, guffawing, and chuckling. One of them, wearing a red kerchief on his head, used his arm to wipe away bits of whatever he'd been drinking as it forced its way out of the sides of his mouth. Another guy with bloodshot eyes and a red face got even redder as he sat down and laughed. "His daughter!" he snorted, banging his drumsticks together as punctuation.

"So you know Annie?" Gord finally asked, still snickering.

"Yes. In Kensington. We play in the band together. We're doing a duet for *The Wizard of Oz* show."

"And it's the pits," Gord said, becoming serious. The band also became solemn.

I must have seemed bewildered because in a moment they all burst out laughing again.

"The pits!" laughed the red-faced drummer, with a *buh-dum-dum* drumroll on the arm of his chair.

It wasn't fair. They worked together as a band so they could make fun of me in sync. They made Matt and Bud look like amateurs.

"I've got to take a Wiz in the Emerald City," the kerchief guy said, walking into the bathroom at the back of the room.

"Ask Dorothy to bring us some more drinks while you're there," the drummer called after him.

I was still perched on the table, standing on the remains of the band's supper. I climbed down off the table and into a pile of broken bottles.

"I just talked to Annie on the phone. She told me to expect you," Gord said. "Though she didn't mention that you'd be coming in through the window."

"I thought it was a bathroom window," I shrugged, scrunching over broken glass.

The concert was amazing. Inside, The Playhouse wasn't as seedy as it was outside. The crowd went nuts over Gord. And I had a seat at a table in the front. I kept looking around, half-expecting to see Chuck, the only other person I knew in Samson. But of course, he wasn't there. Toward the end of the last set, Gord and his band played the Beatles' "She Came in Through the Bathroom Window." They kept looking at me and laughing.

I guess I deserved it.

After the concert, Gord invited me out for a drink and we went to a funky little cafe a few blocks from The Playhouse.

Gord thought that the coincidence of me ending up at his concert was "cosmic."

"A lot of coincidences have been happening to me lately," I said.

He said it was *synchronicity,* which he said meant "meaningful coincidence."

"Things can be connected just because they feel that way to you. There's stuff that science doesn't understand or is just beginning to. It's not all 'for each action there's an equal reaction.' Sometimes there's a kind of energy between things that can't be explained, it just blows your mind. Like why did I happen to be in Samson the same night you were? If you'd been here tomorrow I'd have been in Tollomee, three hundred miles away."

Or, I thought to myself, why did I happen to meet Chuck Ambersoll and talk him into letting me fly all the way out here, only to find out about a plane crash that Uncle Barnard was in?

"My mother would say that these coincidences come from the stars."

"Yeah, maybe they do, but I figure that I'm the thing that makes sense of them. Without me, none of what happens would make as much sense as it does. I think that's the way it is for everybody. You have to be your own sense-maker. That's what my new CD title is about. *Fables from the Blizzard.* We have to make up our own stories about what's really out there 'cause it's like we're in a blizzard all the time and we can't know for sure what we're seeing."

Gord ordered himself another whiskey and said that he could just tell that the cheesecake would be the thing to get.

So I got cheesecake. How wrong can you go with cheesecake?

"Annie said you live with your mother," Gord said. "I was raised by my mother too. My father lived with us, sort of. He was a musician and a rolling stone, that's as in the song, not the band. He tried his best not to gather any moss, or responsibilities, but just to keep moving. But he did come home from time to time. I'd wake up in the morning, and there he'd be, crashed out beside my mom. It was my dad who taught me how to play guitar."

"I don't know anything about my father," I said. "He left, or disappeared, when I was very young. I've been trying to find him."

"Yeah, like the banker's son said, 'all he left me was a loan.' Sorry, bad joke. But it's really too bad about your dad. I know how tough it was for me, and I got to see my dad, once in a while." Gord reached over and helped himself to a huge forkful of cheesecake. "Good," he mumbled, bits of cheesecake falling onto his chin.

Gord offered me a lift home in his band's tour bus. "It ain't much, but we sleep late. And we got lots of munchies, plenty of beer and pop, and a good sound system. And Jake, the drummer, is a wicked card player." They were heading back to Kensington — though it'd be a few weeks before they finally got there. They had a bunch of gigs to play on the way.

I had to get back before that. There was Uncle Barnard and my mom. There was also — what was it called? — school.

"Well, why don't you just come and look at the bus?"

On the way out of the cafe, a few people stopped Gord

to talk to him and to ask if he'd autograph their napkins. Gord quietly said, "Sure," and signed whatever was put in front of him.

If he'd been my dad, I wouldn't have had to forge his signature when I wanted to fly out West. I could have just stuck something in front of him and he'd sign it automatically, in rock star mode.

Of course, if he'd been my dad, I wouldn't have had to trick him.

twenty-seven

How Do The Angels Sleep?

We walked over to where the bus was parked on the far side of The Playhouse. It had obviously once been a school bus.

The kind of bus where a kid could slam another on the head with a saxophone case.

But the bus wasn't yellow anymore. It had been painted with images from Gord Thomas's albums: guitars with wings bursting out of an open mouth. Drums raining down on a cow-filled field. Gord standing on a sunny beach with snow falling just on him. I'd have liked to go to a school that had a bus like this. Gord Thomas High.

We climbed on and Gord led me down the narrow middle aisle. There was a little table and bench seats. Newspapers and music magazines were littered everywhere.

Mixed in were cards, coffee cups, beer bottles, underwear, and a dirty white sports sock. "We did the interior decorating ourselves," Gord said as we walked through. A small oven, a microwave, and a coffee-maker were fitted into panels in the wall. And there was the tantalizing smell of popcorn coming from somewhere.

From behind a little blue curtain it sounded like someone had a chainsaw and was wrestling a pig.

"Jake," Gord said, noticing my look of amazement. "He sleeps as loudly as he plays."

Above Jake's bunk was another small bed with the blue curtain drawn open. "That's where Marty — the bass player — sleeps. But he won't find his way back until the last bar closes."

We passed another set of beds.

"That's my bed there," Gord said. "I have to wear earplugs if I want to get any sleep." He looked toward Jake's bunk. "Drummers!" he laughed.

We continued on to the back of the bus where there was a small lounge with a TV and a computer on one side and a comfortable sofa that was bolted to the floor on the other. Gord lifted a guitar off the sofa and invited me to sit down. A fluffy cat appeared out of nowhere and slid itself beneath Gord's hand. "That's Einstein," Gord said, stroking its long fur. "We found him a couple of months ago. Annie suggested the name."

"Because of the hair?"

"Yeah. Marty calls him 'Electric Chair,' for the same reason."

Gord pushed aside a pile of CDs and cassettes, half of which skidded onto the floor. But he didn't seem to notice.

He pressed a button on the uncovered remote and the lights of an amazing, sleek black stereo turned on and music started. A gravelly voice began singing. It sounded like the guy not only had a chainsaw and a pig but was gargling with some barbed wire, too. But it was beautiful, like late night in a diner.

"Tom Waits," Gord said. "One of my songwriting heroes." He rooted around on the floor for a minute and then produced the CD case. I flipped it open and read the names of the songs.

"So do you want a lift home? All this can be yours . . ." Gord swept his arm expansively over the vista of the messy bus.

Just then there was a noise from the front. Marty staggered in and stumbled down the aisle. I could smell the stale smoke even from the back of the bus. The Playhouse was pretty smoky, but this was worse. As Marty tottered forward, I also began to smell some kind of alcohol radiating off him. It could have been paint stripper or something to dissolve bricks in. The kind of thing that'd make jet fuel seem like chamomile tea.

"Hey, Marty," Gord said, looking at his watch. "You're home early."

"Yeah," Marty said as he wobbled up the little ladder to his bunk. "Now thank you and good night." And he disappeared behind the blue curtain with a loud flop.

"I don't know how he does it. Out drinking every night," Gord commented. "I was too old for that when I was three."

We sat and listened to some more Tom Waits. One song

had a line about how the Devil was just God when he was drunk.

Gord said, "Speak of the Devil," and gestured toward Marty. "Now listen to this next line," he said when another song came on. "I don't know what it means, but it sounds great."

I sat back on the sofa and thought about how amazing it would be to spend some time with Gord and his band on the bus. After a few more songs I finally told Gord, "I really appreciate the offer of staying on the bus, but I really need to get back . . . my mom must be freaking out . . ."

"Another time then . . ."

"OK."

"C'mon, it's late. Let me walk you back to your hotel. Even Marty's in bed."

Chuck was sitting on the front steps of Delilah's Inn, his back against the railing. There was a cool breeze and the sky was bright with stars. I waved bye to Gord.

"I was worried about you," Chuck said.

"But you got my note?"

"Yes, but it's late. And I've had a bad feeling after what happened to my plane."

"Sorry. I wasn't thinking of that." I told him how Gord had taken me to see his tour bus.

"Sounds great," Chuck said. "I'm just looking out for you."

He didn't seem in a hurry to move and so I sat down on the step beside him and leaned back on the railing. For a long time we didn't say much, just looked out at the night. A car with a cracked windshield passed by. A streetlight flickered.

Then Chuck began talking, half to me, half to himself. "I remember a time during the war," he said, "when I was flying on a night like this. I was focused on my mission, trying to make out the coastline, concentrating on my orders. It was cold and clear and when I finally did look out at the sky, my breath just left me, like I'd been hit in the gut. I'd never imagined that there were so many stars. And since this was the southern hemisphere, there were stars that I'd never seen before. It was mind-boggling to realize that there was half a universe that I'd never even thought about."

We were quiet again. I thought about the stars in our half of the universe. I wondered if the stars in the southern hemisphere would say different things to my mother. If they'd sound Australian.

"I can't get my plane fixed out here," Chuck said suddenly. "At least not for a while. I'm figuring on a week. So Doc Tycho is going to send someone out to get us, but not until the day after tomorrow. I'm going out to find me a drink. Might as well. My plane's down. It's what we did in the Force. It's late. You best go back to the room. I'll be up there after not too long." Chuck waited until I went inside and then went off in search of the last open bar in Samson.

We wouldn't get home until the day after tomorrow? I was worried about leaving my mother for so long.

And the trouble that would be waiting for me at home had just doubled.

I went up to the room. The door was slightly ajar.

Probably the busybody woman from behind the desk had been snooping, on the pretext that she was giving us new towels or fixing up the bowls of scented flowers. "Hello?" I said as I walked into the dark room.

There was someone there.

Only it wasn't the busybody woman.

twenty-eight

Search and Rescue

As soon as I entered the room, a strong smell jumped out from behind the air-freshener disaster and hit me square in the nose.

Industrial-strength Nicholas Copper, now with paint thinner.

He was sitting on a chair in the dark with his legs stretched out onto a bed. How had he figured out that we were staying here?

"Kid, I know who you are. I've been doing my own checking," he snarled at the floor. "Barnard Isaacson is your uncle. You've been playing dumb." He sat up and spat at the wall. "You and your friend, Chuck. You stop sticking your fat noses where it's none of your damn business." He stood up and stepped toward me, pushing his face close to mine. His breath was the rocket fuel of the pig god. Copper wasn't a friendly, goofy kind of drunk like Marty. He was a mean, dangerous drunk. I wondered if he'd always been like that. "Get out of here or it'll be more than your plane we'll beat the crap out of." He shoved his flat palm against my shoulder and I fell down against the door.

I scrambled up and ran down the hall, down the steps, and out into the dark street. I scanned the sidewalks for Chuck, but he wasn't there. I kept running. My breathing was loud in the empty street. I didn't look around to see if Nicholas Copper was behind me. He'd said, "We'll" beat the crap out of you. I didn't fancy running into the other part of that "we," whoever they were. I'd seen what they'd done to the plane.

A truck was pulled over in front of a gas station. The driver was walking out of the booth, shaking his head. "Ex, excuse me," I panted. "I need, I need a ride. Can you . . ."

"As long as you dint rob no bank," the driver chuckled.

"No, I . . ."

"Get in. Where you headed? You tell me the story."

We drove for a while. First along one of those streets filled with bright lights and car dealerships. Then onto the highway. I was out of breath and didn't say much. I still hadn't come down from the scare.

Must have been how Matt felt when I decked him with my sax.

Right.

I felt strangely light, traveling in the dark cab of a big truck without anything but my clothes. And my rapier sharp wit.

Right.

But really I only had about ten dollars and no change of clothes. I'd left my luggage (an overstuffed backpack) at the bed-and-breakfast. The truck driver didn't say anything. It was beginning to rain and he kept his eyes narrowed, staring at the slick strip of road that appeared before us. He also drank from an enormous plastic coffee cup. This was why he'd stopped at the first roadside truck stop after we'd been driving for just an hour.

"The can back at the station in Samson was busted," he explained as he pulled into the truck stop. "Stretch your legs if you like."

I climbed down from the rig. About thirty trucks were parked around us: huge, sleeping dinosaurs. There was a payphone near the gas pumps. I had a bad feeling. Actually I was full of bad feelings. I wanted to check on Barnard and let my mom know where I was. In case something happened.

I called our personal number.

"Barnard. Is that you? Are you OK? Where are you? Do you need help?" My mother sounded frantic.

"Mom, it's Alex."

"Alex, are you all right? Oh my lord, where are you? Barnard's gone. He left talking about crazy things. He was going to do something crazy. Come home right away — you've got to help him."

It seemed that she had no idea I was hundreds of miles away. She still thought I'd gone to school and stayed at a friend's overnight.

"Tell that man with the plane to bring you home. We'll sort all the rest out later. Clare told me all about it."

Of course, Annie's mom told her.

"It's almost the sixteenth. The day after tomorrow it'll

be twelve years after . . . after — I can't tell you now, but Barnard is going to do something crazy. You have to get to him before . . . he gets hurt."

I heard a squeal of tires and looked up to see a car with a broken windshield speed into the truck stop and park halfway onto the sidewalk. The truck driver had just walked out of the main building when someone got out of the car and walked quickly, threateningly, up to him. Nicholas Copper! No! He must have followed me out of the hotel and then tracked me in his car until I got into the truck, then gunned it in his jalopy, keeping up with us until we stopped. I felt a thousand rabbits thumping against my ribcage.

"I have to go," I said — unhelpfully — to my mother as I slammed the receiver down. I ducked behind the gas pumps, slipped behind a row of parked trucks, then hopped a fence and ran across a field bristling with stubble. I fell a few times on the uneven ground littered with slick rocks. I came down hard once on the prickly stubble, grazing my face and hands. But I kept running, constantly looking over my shoulder. Behind me, the glare of the truck stop was fading into the distance. There was nothing ahead of me.

I crashed into a barbed wire fence at full speed and cut my chest and forehead. I didn't stop, but kept going a little way along the fence until I found a metal gate. I climbed over it. Then I crossed a path and climbed over another gate and kept running. If Copper had followed me this far, there was no telling what he might do. He'd pulled a gun on Chuck and me when we first went to his place. That should have told us something.

I began to slow down, resting every now and then, bending over, my hands on my knees, breathing deeply. It started to rain even harder. I saw a light in the distance and thought I could see the dim shape of a barn beside it. I headed in that direction. I'd hide in the barn, catch my breath. Listen for signs of Copper.

The barn door was stuck. There was just enough room for me to squeeze through. Inside I could make out heaps of hay, a tractor, a few sacks of something, and a tire. Some small thing scuttling. I hoped it wasn't rats. Given my circumstances, I could put up with mice, maybe even an owl or bats. But not rats. I sat down on a pile of hay. Once I'd stopped moving, the sounds got louder. The rain. My own breathing. My heart. A rustling in the barn. I listened for any trace of Nicholas Copper.

Nothing.

I waited in the barn for hours. I sat like an owl, swiveling my head at the slightest sound, ready to move at a moment's notice. Finally, cold and exhausted, I lay back on a bale of hay. The sound of the rain was hypnotic and I soon fell asleep.

The next sound was the most completely terrifying thing that I'd ever heard. I'd rolled off the bale of hay and was wedged in between it and the huge wheel of the tractor. The rain had stopped and I was woken by an electronic ringing in the half-light of dawn. I almost hit the roof. I wished that I had, since instead I hit my head on the tractor trying to sit up.

I had no idea what the sound was or where exactly it was coming from. Eventually I figured out that its source was beneath the tractor. I had to dig through a carpet of hay to get to it. It was a small black cell phone. If it had been a horror movie, I'd have answered the phone and it would have been Nicholas Copper saying something awful.

I didn't dare answer it.

Instead, I stuffed the phone under the hay bale, muffling the ringing sound. I didn't want anyone to find me there. It was early morning and, this being a farm, there could be people up. I could imagine the farmer saying, "Dang. So *that's* where I dropped my gol'darn cell phone," and then tromping into the barn only to find me there.

When the ringing stopped, I took the phone out from under the bale. In my pocket I had the envelope with Chuck's directions to Delilah's Inn. He'd written down the phone number at the top. I dialed and asked the irritated and sleepy voice on the other end to get me Chuck's room.

Chuck was also sleepy and irritated when he picked up the phone.

"Who the hell is this?"

"Copper's after me," I said.

"Alex! Are you OK? Where in the blazes are you? Are you safe?"

"I think so." Copper couldn't have known where I was hiding.

"Good," Chuck said. "I had my own run-in with one of his friends. Or *he* had a run-in with me and I left him on the floor. But why doesn't he leave you out of it?"

Good question.

I explained about being chased.

"Find out where you are and I'll come get you. Doc Tycho called me in the middle of last night — early this morning. Anyway, he managed to talk someone into lending him a long-range chopper and he'll be here in a few hours."

"I have to get home. There's a family emergency." It wasn't the time to get into the fact that his Barnard Isaacson was my Uncle Barnard. "I'll call you as soon as I find out where I am."

Through the opening in the barn door, I could see the back of a farmhouse. It was too early to knock on the door. Besides what would they say if a disheveled and bloody-faced teenager appeared at their door not knowing where he was?

I crept out of the barn and looked around. There was nothing but fields. No helpful Munchkins to tell me where I was. And certainly no well-maintained yellow brick road with helpful signage telling me where to go. I remembered the old joke about how to find out what time it is in the middle of the night. You phone someone up and they say, "Don't you realize it's 3:30 (or whatever time it is) in the morning!!!" Then you say, "Thanks," and hang up. But it wouldn't work for *where* you are.

Anyway, I thought, the good thing is that I seem to have lost Nicholas Copper. Then I heard the rumble of a car on the dirt road. I ducked behind the barn and peered around. It wasn't Copper. It was a blue pickup truck. It stopped at the mailbox in front of the house. A big hairy arm poked out the window and stuffed a few letters into the mailbox, lifted the little red flag on its side, and reversed back down the road.

Bingo.

How do you find out where you are without asking?

You look at the address on a letter. Ron and Jenny McCurdy's letters were all addressed 1357 3rd Street South, Maxville. Where exactly that was, I'd let Chuck figure out. I dialed Delilah's Inn.

I was to wait a couple of hours. But I didn't want the McCurdys to find me — I didn't want to get into the whole story. Instead, I headed out across a field. There was a small clump of trees where I could hide. I'd hear the helicopter. Of course, so would the McCurdys but by then it wouldn't matter. I'd be in the helicopter flying back to Auntie Em and Kansas.

And, hopefully, apple pie.

There was a large fallen maple a little way into the trees. I sat with my back against it, looking out at the field, puzzling over what my mother had said. What could Uncle Barnard be up to? Why was twelve years so important? And twelve years after what? But then I knew. It was twelve years after the crash of his frogplane. Also twelve years after my father disappeared. Everything was happening at once. I had to get home. At some point in my wondering, I heard the helicopter.

I ran out into the middle of the mucky field toward the buzzing, hopping over puddles left by the rain of the night before. The helicopter was coming from my left. In order to see it I had to look directly into the sun. Then it was overhead. I waved my hands frantically — as if they might mistake me for a cow in the field. A door opened and Chuck threw down a rope ladder. The chopper hung unsteadily above me. I grabbed at the ladder and hoisted myself up, scrambling until I got my feet on the rungs.

Someone was using my stomach as a trampoline. I tried not to look down. Or to fall. When I got to the top, Chuck reached out and held onto my arms. Then I was in, sitting on the floor while Chuck hauled in the ladder. He closed the door and we swooped up and away from the McCurdys, who were standing in front of their side door, shielding their eyes, looking into the sky with no idea of what was going on.

If they could have heard me, I would have yelled, "Take me to your leader. Meep meep."

Dr. Tycho was sitting in the front of the helicopter beside the pilot. She had brown hair tied in a long braid, but beyond that I couldn't tell much about her. She was wearing big sunglasses, a black beret, and huge headphones. Every now and then she would mutter something into her headset.

"So we're definitely on to something with this Nicholas Copper fellow, yah?" Dr. Tycho shouted above the noise of the helicopter. "It starts to get interesting, no?"

"We are going back to Kensington, right? I need to get home." I didn't feel like joking. "My Uncle Barnard . . ."

"Uncle Barnard!" Chuck echoed. "I thought he might be related to you. Your Uncle Barnard is Barnard Isaacson."

I explained that I was going to tell them.

Eventually.

I was glad that the helicopter was so loud. The noise was like a shield.

"He's not well," I said, hoping Chuck would understand why I hadn't told them Barnard was my uncle.

"The security guard back at the Kensington airport told us he wasn't entirely right. Your uncle made quite an impression on him a few weeks back. Apparently, he was trying to get access to a restricted area."

"He's in trouble. I have to get home."

"We'd like to talk to him, too. We'll get there soon as we can in this chopper. It'll be sometime this afternoon. We'll have to stop a few times to refuel. These things can do about 400 miles max. So you might as well sit back and enjoy the view as best you can."

"But it looks like you got cut pretty bad, no? It wasn't Copper, I hope?" Dr. Tycho said. He passed Chuck a first-aid kit from a pocket in front of him.

I explained about my run-in with the fence and the ground. "I put up quite a fight."

twenty-nine

Search and Rescue 2.0

For much of the way back to the Kensington airport, I was too wound up and exhausted to either sleep or enjoy the view. When I finally did drift off, I had a dream in which my mother (blonde and thin) floated around the house offering me my dinner on a tray. I was hardly comfortable slumped against the side of the helicopter but, thankfully, I received no cell phone wake-up calls from under the seat. When we landed, Kensingston airport was a busy place — the Aeronautical Society was meeting today and many members had just flown in.

"It's how I happened to run into Sue here," Dr. Tycho said. "An old friend. An excellent pilot. Yes, Sue?"

The pilot nodded. She was still at the controls, writing some notes in her flight book.

As soon as I was in the terminal, I called home. My mother thanked a whole pile of stars that I was back but said there was still no sign of Barnard. "I'll go over to his apartment," I told her.

"Clare — Annie's mom — already checked several times. He's not there."

"I'll go anyway. Maybe I can figure something out."

"Hurry."

Chuck and I drove over in his car. I pounded on Uncle Barnard's door.

"Uncle Barnard!"

No answer.

Chuck suggested that we find the super and explain that it was an emergency, that Barnard could be in danger.

"You mean like a heart attack?" the super asked after we hammered on his door.

"Yes. He's sick. We need to check right away."

"Mr. Isaacson — he's not quite well in the head?" the super half-asked, half-commented as he opened the door, motioning to the fish that hung there. "We've had complaints."

I rushed in and searched the apartment. Uncle Barnard wasn't there. The frog painting was gone, too. On his kitchen table, mixed in with the onions, an old shoe, piles of books and papers, and some plates encrusted with dried spaghetti, I found some paper airplanes.

"Let's check by the river."

We left the bewildered super standing in Uncle Barnard's front hall and ran down the stairs to Chuck's car.

Uncle Barnard wasn't at the river either, but the frog

painting was propped up on the bench. A large hole was ripped out of its center.

We saw something across the river.

Uncle Barnard was hunched behind a tree, shaking.

"Uncle Barnard. Uncle Barnard." He didn't seem to hear. I stepped into the cold water and sloshed through the weeds near the edge of the river. It was painfully cold on my legs. Chuck called me back but I kept going. As I got deeper, the river closed around me, my wet clothes pulling me down. I was forced to rush to my uncle in slow motion.

When the water reached up to my shoulders I began to swim. I half-staggered up to the opposite bank and knelt in front of Uncle Barnard.

He was sobbing.

"I tried to. But I was scared."

"Tried to do w-w-what?" I started shaking as well.

"We agreed to. We said we would. But I was scared. I couldn't."

I put my hand on Uncle Barnard's shoulder. He was sopping wet and very cold.

By this time, Chuck had driven his car around to the other side of the riverbank.

"We need to get him home," I called. Together we maneuvered Barnard into the back seat of Chuck's car. Uncle Barnard didn't wave his arms around. He hardly moved, except for the shaking.

"Looks like shell shock to me. Guys in the war, they looked like this," Chuck said.

". . . the sky . . . frog . . . no . . ." Uncle Barnard kept muttering as if he were having a bad dream. "MY PLANE!" he shouted.

"Where, where is your plane?"

We drove back to my house and walked him straight into my room. I felt like a Freezie and so right away I changed into a dry outfit. Chuck stripped off Uncle Barnard's sopping clothes and put him into my bed, while I put his things in the dryer. Barnard lay shaking under the covers until he finally went to sleep. After a while, Chuck wrote his cell phone number on a little slip of paper and told me to call if I needed to. He said he'd be back tomorrow, to check on Uncle Barnard and to see how things were going. He gave me a quick salute and left.

I didn't say much to my mother. She'd obviously heard us bringing Barnard in, but when I stood at her door and told her I was back and that we'd found Barnard, she began to cry. I didn't want to have to explain everything, or give her the chance to yell at me about being away, so even after Uncle Barnard went to sleep, I continued to look busy. Then the phone rang and she answered it. This meant I could stop walking in and out of my room as if I were carrying urgent messages from the Roman Emperor. It also meant that I could check my e-mail. It'd been a few days.

There were all sorts of messages. And there was a strange e-mail from the bouncing guy:

From: bounce@bounce.net

To: alexisaacson@hotmail.com

Subject: Re: Bouncing

I've bounced toward the sky. Like Icarus I tried to get too close to the sun and I fell back. But I have rebounded. Now it is time for me to get close to the son again. I hope I will not burn.

-Dadulus

I remember puzzling over this. I remember reading some websites about the helicopter I'd just flown in. And I remember searching for my father. But I don't remember falling asleep on top of my computer. I guess it wasn't surprising considering what had happened over the last day and when it had happened.

"Newton!" Uncle Barnard shouted in his sleep. I sat up and looked around, trying to figure out where I was. I'd slept all night. "Newton!" Barnard called out again, and then woke with a start. I went over to his bed. He was breathing heavily. Then he began talking frantically, gesturing violently with his arms as if he was trying to keep rain from hitting the ground. "Alex, your father, your father, he thinks like me and you know how you found me. If he's thinking what I was thinking then I think he . . . we've got to help him, we've got to find him before it is too late — if it isn't too late already — when is it and what time?"

I tried to console him, while at the same time I tried to keep my self calm. He was finally talking about my father even if he was raving. It sounded urgent but I didn't know whether to believe what he was saying. "It's OK, Uncle. It's OK," I kept repeating in a soothing voice. But he was unconsolable.

"It is true. It is true. We must help your father. I should

have told you before. It is time now. We must help. We must go there."

There was a knock on the bedroom door. It was Clare.

"Alex, I've come to help with your mother. Is everything all right?" She gestured toward Barnard. "Is there anything I can do to help?"

"We have to go. We have to go to his father. A hurry. We must go." Uncle Barnard swung himself over the edge of the bed. He was quite a sight — a big, shaking, waving man wearing my underwear.

"He says we have to help my father." It didn't feel real to be talking about my father as if he existed in the same world as me. As if we could go to him. As if anything my uncle was saying could be true.

"We must go. I am not sick. I know what I say." Uncle Barnard stood up and looked around for his clothes.

I passed him a dressing gown and told him his clothes were in the dryer.

"I can look after your mother, Alex," Clare said. "But would it be possible for Annie to help, too? I've got work . . ."

I didn't want Annie to know about my family, but there seemed to be little choice.

"OK," I said after a pause.

"She'll understand," Clare said. "I'll get your clothes," she said to Barnard.

As soon as she left, I turned to my uncle. "You know where my father is? Where? Why didn't you tell me? What kind of help does he need?"

If he knew what he was saying, there'd be no more running away. He'd have to answer to me.

thirty

Not the Emerald City Regional Detention Center

I phoned Chuck. An hour later, Chuck, Barnard, and I were in Chuck's car barreling through small towns on the way to the place where my father was — as far as we could make out from my uncle's hyperactive and confusing directions. If directions were a cat, then Uncle Barnard's directions were a cat in a bathtub. Which made all these small towns the mouse-shaped soap that kept slipping out from under his wet and frantic paws. Uncle Barnard knew and didn't know where my father was. We were trying to recreate a route that he'd once taken twelve years ago. As far as we could tell, my father was living somewhere in the countryside, outside a town of which Uncle Barnard couldn't quite remember the name. But, he assured us, he could find it.

I sat in the back seat. Barnard sat up front, waving his

arms, pointing to turn-offs that Chuck had just driven past, muttering, weeping, or calling out every few minutes.

The experience was completely awful. Now that the moment had actually arrived, I was scared to meet my father. Uncle Barnard's behavior was bewildering and worrisome. And in order to follow Barnard's directions, Chuck had to drive as if he'd flunked out of stuntman school.

We stopped to fill up the gas tank. Chuck and I walked over to get some pop from a machine. I must have looked exactly like I felt because Chuck smiled sympathetically at me and said, "Son, we were sent out to bomb places knowing much less than this." He was trying to be reassuring.

I didn't feel reassured.

Though Barnard was spluttering directions and muttering constantly, we weren't able to find out much about my father. He had run away and dropped out of sight twelve years before, right after Uncle Barnard's frogplane crashed. But why he'd disappeared we weren't able to find out from Barnard.

When we asked he began to panic, to breathe so quickly that he started hyperventilating and acting even crazier. He tried to open the car door and get out.

While we were still driving.

We decided to leave the questions until we'd reached our destination.

As we drove, I looked out the window, imagining that every man I saw was my father. I hadn't thought about what I expected to happen, or even what I'd say once I found him. It's not like imagining what you would do with the money if you won the lottery. There were some real creepy-looking characters walking down the street. There were also some men who looked perfectly normal, but I couldn't imagine what I could possibly say to any of them. And what if my father was a total jerk or as nutty as Barnard?

I didn't need anyone else to look after.

"We must get there. I want it not to be too late. Chuck, you must hurry now!" Barnard banged his fist on the dashboard and began to gnaw furiously on his lower lip.

We understood from what Barnard had said that twelve years ago he and my father had made some kind of pact to try something dangerous. It had something to do with the frogplane. Barnard gave us a jumbled account mixing mythology, astronomy, and legends from around the world. There was some connection between the position of the planet Jupiter and their flight. Jupiter was the sky god, and twelve earth years were the same as one year on Jupiter. There was also something else about frogs in Native American belief, and the distance in light-years to some star. But the main thing was that it sounded like my father and Barnard had each planned to build another frogplane. In which case Barnard worried that it would crash like the first one, and someone might get killed again. It didn't work like it does on cartoons, where one bash on the head makes you crazy and the second makes you better again. In real life, if the first time was bad, the next time might be worse.

"Stop now. We must walk," Barnard said as we rounded a nondescript bend in the road. Chuck turned around and looked at me skeptically, but I just shrugged. What else could we do but trust that Barnard wasn't leading us on a wild goose chase? Or, in this case, a wild frog chase.

Chuck stopped the car on the shoulder of the road. On one side of the road were farmers' fields. On the other were dense woods. We followed Barnard as he plunged into the woods. The pine trees were close together. The branches were sharp and their needles were prickly. We had to hold our hands in front of our faces to avoid them.

Eventually we got to the other side of the woods, to the edge of a large field filled with neat rows of vegetables. Scattered throughout the field were workers in blue overalls tending to the crop. Quite far away, on the other side of the field, were many trampolines with people bouncing on them. It looked like some sort of gymnastics camp. As we got closer, we saw that the trampolinists were all men. They were dressed identically in dark blue pants and blue shirts under blue vests. It seemed like some sort of recreational activity for prison inmates. The whole time, I'd imagined that we were on our way to the Emerald City. But this was a horse of a different color. These were the inmates of Oz and they were kept in the Emerald City Regional Detention Center by the Warden of Oz.

Even though some of the men were laughing, it all looked very serious. They weren't concentrating on doing tricks — somersaults and fancy falls — the kind of things that trampolinists usually do. They were bouncing straight up and down as if they were trying to bounce higher and higher. As if they could actually bounce into the sky or up toward the sun. It was just like what that last e-mail had said: "I've bounced toward the sky," and "it is time for me to get close to the son again."

The e-mails! My father had been sending me messages all this time! I'd been talking to my father and I didn't even know it. Not that I'd had any idea what he'd been talking about. I wondered which one of the trampolining men was my father. They all looked quite alike. Not only were they dressed identically, but they had the same long hair that fluttered around them as they bounced.

There were several men standing beside each trampoline, waiting for a turn. At a certain moment, all the trampolining men suddenly stopped bouncing and fell to the surface of their trampolines. They slipped off and, a moment later, a new set of men were bounding toward the sky.

"What the hell is this place?" Chuck hissed.

"They are Bouncing Men," Barnard said.

"I can see that. But what is this? Some kind of jail?"

"It is like a monastery, a retreat. The Bouncing Men live simple lives here. They work the fields. They meditate and bounce here. It is their choice." Barnard walked quickly forward, toward the trampolines. "Where is Newton Isaacson? We need to be talking to him."

"Who are you? Why do you disturb us? Our bouncing must not be disturbed." A man with long gray hair spoke from the gathering crowd of blue men. Bouncing men dropped from their trampolines and surrounded us. "This place is not for you. It is for Bouncing Men only."

"We didn't mean to disturb you." I said. "We came here to find my father." A look of quick panic came over the Bouncing Men. Some took a step back from us, as if we were hostile dogs. "My father's name is —"

"The place of the Bouncing Men is a place of peace," the gray-haired man interrupted. "It is a place away from the world. It is a place without fathers. You must leave. This is not a place where someone comes to be found."

"His father may be in danger," Chuck said.

"He has sent me messages," I said. It wasn't only the Bouncing Man who looked surprised. Chuck and Barnard looked at me, too.

"Come with me," the Bouncing Man said sternly.

He led us into an old brick house surrounded by concrete-block buildings. We all sat down around a large boardroom table in what would have been the living room of the house. I was silent. I noticed a computer in the corner of the room. Barnard was quiet but twitchy.

"We're looking for Newton Isaacson," Chuck said.

"The Bouncing Men leave their names behind when they enter this place."

"Right," Chuck said. "But I'm sure you know who they are."

"The Place of the Bouncing Men is a place where men come to leave the world behind."

"I understand," Chuck said. "But—"

"But my father contacted me," I interrupted. "He didn't leave the world behind."

"We are all at different stages of development as Bouncing Men," the gray-haired man explained. "Men come here to leave what holds them to the earth. What weighs heavily on them. We try to bound beyond, to leap toward freedom."

"You're telling me that you guys are trying to fly?" Chuck was beginning to sound irritated.

"In a way, yes. A spiritual flight. A flight from that which makes us heavy."

"By trampolining?"

"It is a form of meditation. We learn to leap beyond our thoughts and the restrictions of our earthly emotions."

Barnard stood up suddenly, knocking his chair backward. His arms began to wave around and he shook his head back and forth. He began to speak very loudly. "I know he is here. Something of danger may be happening. Let us see him."

Then Chuck also got to his feet, and so I stood up too, not to be left out of this standing non-ovation.

"We don't want to involve the police," I said. It was the kind of thing that they always said on TV shows. It seemed that, these days, I had a direct cable connection.

The gray-haired Bouncing Man remained seated, looking at us without expression. Then finally he said, "I will take you to him."

He led us through the Bouncing Men compound — numerous, identical, low concrete-block buildings. Then he pointed to a building at the edge.

"He is there."

We ran to the door. Chuck opened it, and he and Barnard plunged in. The door swung shut behind them. I hesitated. I was excited and terrified, not knowing what — or who — I might find. Then I pulled open the door and went in.

thirty-one

Keeping Secrets

Chuck and Barnard were at the end of a little entrance hall. I caught up with them as they walked through an open doorway into a large, mostly empty space. The outside door banged closed. At the far end, a series of beds lined the walls. There was hardly anything else in the room. The floor and walls were concrete. Dim light was provided by a few lightbulbs hanging from the ceiling. It looked like a jail or else a set from an old movie about the army. Near the back wall, a man was sitting on a bed, his elbows on his knees, his hands clasping his head.

"Newton!" Barnard called out. His voice boomed in the empty dormitory. His heavy footsteps echoed as he strode quickly forward. A windmill on important business.

The man turned to look at him. Then he looked down at the floor again. "Go away. Please go away."

"Newton, it is Barnard."

The man stood up. "Barnard . . ."

Barnard jerked forward and grabbed him. He pulled the man toward him. My father, much smaller than Barnard, was surrounded in his embrace, a rag doll clutched by its overenthusiastic owner. After a moment's hesitation, my father put his arms around Barnard. They both began to cry.

"I couldn't do it. I couldn't do it," my father sobbed.

"I also did not do it, brother. I also could not fly again. I did not even make another plane." Barnard, though crying, sounded like the strong one.

I didn't know what to do. Here I was, after twelve years, standing on the other side of the room from my father and we weren't speaking. No matter how nervous I was, I knew that I was finally at the end of the yellow brick road and it was time to talk to the Wizard.

I started walking toward him. I felt like I was falling, just like when I looked into Uncle Barnard's frog painting. "Dad," I said, the name sounding strange. "It's Alex."

His arms dropped.

"Alex." He slipped free from Barnard's still-hugging arms. We stood facing each other. My father wiped his eyes with the back of his hands and rubbed his nose, sniffling.

I had been harboring the hope that my father would be big enough to make things better. As big as he'd loomed in my mind. Certainly as big and vigorous as my uncle, if not so eccentric.

Not for one moment had I imagined that my father

would be a thin, whispering man the same size as me. I never believed that my father wouldn't know what to do when we met. It would have been easier if he'd been a drinking loudmouth with a whole bunch of girlfriends. What he'd do might not be the right thing, but at least he'd *do* something.

I felt that the curtains had been pulled back and, Wizard of Oz-like, my father had been exposed as a bumbling old man far away from home, trying to put up a strong front. I could see that my father was trying to pull himself together in order to look good for me — his son. I think we both knew it was pretty impossible to look good enough to make up for twelve years.

We stood under the dim lightbulbs. My father looked at me, then down at his worn brown slippers. He ran his fingers through his scraggly ginger hair. The same red hair that I'd had buzzed short.

I wanted to ask him, "Why?" Why everything. But it was too big for words. I felt my insides sink.

I said nothing.

"He's safe, Barnard. Why don't we leave them to talk?" Chuck motioned toward the door.

"You'll be OK, Newton? You'll be fine, brother?" Barnard didn't want to leave, but Chuck guided him out. My father was silent, waiting for the heavy metal door to slam shut.

He lifted his arms toward me as if he was thinking of hugging me.

I didn't want to be hugged. I sat down on a bed across from him.

My father lowered himself onto his own bed.

Silence.

"I was hoping that you would find me," he finally said, "but I was also hoping . . . that you wouldn't." His voice was soft. I could hardly hear him. "I'm a mess now." He looked at the floor.

It was true. He didn't look like much. I thought back to what kind of person I'd imagined was sending the e-mails. Someone full of energy. Clever. Up for a joke.

"They were funny," I said. "The e-mails."

"I thought you'd get them. You were always clever."

Yeah. Smart with building blocks and drool. It had been awhile since he'd seen me. I could feel anger and hurt welling up inside me.

But I wanted things to sound normal. "Thanks," I said, trying to sound relaxed. There was another uncomfortable silence. I was getting frustrated.

"But why didn't you just call me? Or let me know it was you?" I blurted out.

"Look, Alex, I . . ." My father shifted on the bed and the springs creaked.

Pause.

"There are things you don't know."

"I know you left me and mom."

"Other things."

"You mean like the plane crash?"

He stood up and walked quickly across the room. He stood facing the wall, breathing hard and quick.

"You heard about it from Barnard?" He turned toward me. "We didn't ever think it would crash. We were sure it was safe. Otherwise, we would never have . . ." He looked like he wanted to bounce the thoughts away.

But I'd had enough of waiting to find answers.

"You mean the girl?"

He covered his face with his hands. He didn't speak for a long time.

Then in a whisper: "We couldn't imagine that anything could go wrong . . . We . . . It was my fault. I should have protected her." His voice broke. His narrow shoulders shook with sobs. "My own daughter. My own . . . Alison."

The fist of the heavyweight champion of the world came blasting out of the past and hit me hard. I couldn't breathe. I had no lungs. And what I'd just been told came crashing through me.

My father had gone up in the frogplane with Barnard and his own daughter.

I'd had a sister and she'd flown the plane.

I'd had a sister and she'd flown the plane.

That's what all this was about. When were they planning on telling me? When did they think I should know? Why didn't Barnard tell me? Why did he keep this from me? And my mother, why didn't . . . oh, God.

"Did my mother know?" I snapped. "Did my mother know that you were going to put my sister in that — in your goddamn frogplane?"

"Alex . . ." my father began, half in pain, half trying to be soothing.

"Just tell me, did my mother know?"

He stood there motionless, not looking at anything. Then finally:

"Yes."

My bones melted. I fell back onto the bed. My insides were the Grand Canyon filled with fire. All this time my mother had been keeping this from me. Had kept Alison from me. For twelve years she'd hidden this secret from me and I'd had to live like I was falling through the sky without knowing anything. Never mind my goddamn father, I had to talk to my mother.

I ran across the dormitory, shoved open the heavy door, and stormed outside.

thirty-two

The Huge Hole

I rushed around the Bouncing Men camp looking for Chuck and Barnard. I needed to get back to Kensington to talk to my mother.

I ran over to the main building, over to the field of trampolines, past the old-fashioned water pump and fields filled with vegetables. My head was pounding. There was a horrible accident in there and my thoughts were pushing and shoving to get a closer look. They were elbowing the insides of my head.

Why didn't anyone tell me about Alison? They were protecting each other, the three of them, the slime. All this time, Barnard knew where my father was. And they all knew about the plane crash and about Alison.

Alison.

Alex and Alison.

Imagine someone saying that. Someone shouting it down the street to call us home for supper.

Alison and I walking to school together. Sitting beside each other on the couch watching TV. Alison brushing her hair, dressing to go out with a boyfriend. Alison bugging me about Annie. Looking after our mother together. Of course, if Alison were alive, then probably my mother wouldn't have been stuck in bed, wouldn't have stuck herself in bed, wouldn't have left the world. Maybe my father would even have been around, joking with his nutty brother, building crazy contraptions and flying them around the countryside outside of Kensington.

The crazy contraptions. Barnard and my father putting Alison in the frogplane. The three of them cramped in the little cockpit as the frogplane falls from the sky, crashes into the ground. The burning plane, my father and Barnard struggling with the wreckage trying to get Alison out of her seat. She is floppy, twisted. Barnard on the scorched grass raising his arms and howling at the sky. My father falling to his knees, covering his face. And my mom picking up the phone in her room at home, hearing my father's voice shaking. She falls down onto the bed, closes her eyes. "No. No. No," she says. "It isn't true." She stays like this all day. Then the stars come out and she squeezes her eyes shut and tries to be far away. Far away across the galaxy, millions of years before the plane crash. And she just stays in bed. And I'm there somewhere, just a little kid wandering about, calling for my mother, not knowing what's going on. Not knowing that my sister has fallen from the sky. Is a rag doll in a heap of twisted burning metal.

I found Chuck and Barnard walking alongside a stream.

"Let's get the hell out of here."

"You all right?" Chuck asked.

"I just need to get home. I have to talk to my mother."

Barnard wasn't happy about it but we left my father and headed home. This time I sat in the front beside Chuck.

I'd had enough of Uncle Barnard's craziness. Now I would wave my arms around and act however I wanted to. "He's not going anywhere. We — you — can come back and visit him another time. You know where he is."

Uncle Barnard didn't argue. He just stared out the window. Or perhaps *at* the window. He didn't really seem to be staring at anything.

"Now I don't want to pry or anything, but is everything OK, Alex?" Chuck was trying to be sensitive.

"Yes," I said and looked at the front window for the rest of the ride home.

When the car scrunched into the driveway, Barnard hopped out of it before it had fully stopped. He ran straight in.

"Thanks," I said to Chuck.

"If you need to talk . . ."

"Yeah. Thanks," I said. "And thanks for the ride."

"They're shell-shocked, Alex. Keep a cool head so you don't get it too, right?"

"OK."

"Call me soon and let me know how things are going." Chuck nodded his head and did this thing with his eyebrows to let me know that he knew heavy stuff was happening. And that perhaps he'd been through some of his own.

And lived to tell the tale.

Shell shock — it's not contagious! Besides what did they have to be shocked about? They'd known all about the crash for years. I was the one who should be shocked — shocked to find out about Alison.

I knew that I had to confront my mother, but by the time I was walking up the front steps, I wasn't quite so angry or certain. I didn't have any idea what it would be like inside. And I didn't want a scene. I knew from bitter experience that my mother would just clam up and I'd be nowhere again, knowing nothing.

But it *was* like she was shell-shocked. Shocked by the world. Shocked into jumping away from the subject of my father. And as for Uncle Barnard, that went without saying.

Everything was calm when I opened the door. Considering how my uncle had bolted in, I'd have expected to see cartoon speed lines still in the air. But soft classical music was playing in the kitchen. Guitars and violins. Annie's mom was at the sink, drying some dishes. Something good-smelling was baking. Bread. Or maybe cake. It almost seemed like a normal house.

"Hi," Clare said softly, smiling gently. "Your uncle's in the bedroom with your mother."

I stood in front of the almost-closed door for maybe five deep breaths. Then I went in.

Barnard was sitting on a folding chair on the far side of the room. The chair looked small and fragile underneath him. Uncle Barnard's body was in the room but his mind seemed to be elsewhere. My mom was lying on her back looking up at the ceiling. It was as if nothing had happened. They could have been waiting for their appointment at the doctor's office.

Or their execution.

I stood in the middle of the room.

"Alex," my mother said without moving.

"Are you all right?" I said.

"Yes. Clare and Annie have been wonderful."

"Good."

Pause.

"I've been to see Dad."

Her eyes filled with tears. "I . . . I know."

I felt a rush of anger. What else did she know? Everyone seemed to be talking to everyone else except me. It was my time to act. I'd had enough of taking care of everyone else's problems.

My mom was still looking up at the skylight, not at me. She'll look now, I thought. I stood over her. "All this time, did you know where he was?"

"No, Alex. I had no idea." She was beginning to sob.

But maybe she'd known all along who I could ask.

"Did you know that Uncle Barnard knew?"

"No!" she cried. "I didn't know about anything." Her chest was heaving as she strained for breath.

"But you knew about Alison." I couldn't help raising my voice. "Why didn't you tell me about Alison? Why didn't you tell me?" I shouted.

"Alex, I . . ." was all that came out and she turned very red. She began gasping. Her arms started to shake. She was having some kind of attack.

"Mom!" I didn't know what to do. "Clare!"

Clare rushed in.

"She can't breathe!"

"Oh, God!" She put her palm against my mother's forehead and rubbed it. She spoke softly. "It's OK, Marcia. It's OK. It's OK."

I picked up the phone from the night table and dialed 911.

My mother kept struggling and gasping for what felt like hours.

Then there were sirens. Then firefighters stomped through the door. "We're in here," Clare called out. "In the bedroom."

A firefighter in big boots and a long black jacket rushed up to my mother and began examining her. By this time she wasn't moving. He leaned over her and began listening.

"She's not breathing," he said to another firefighter. He stuck his fingers into her mouth. "It's not blocked."

The other firefighter put a mask over her face and began pumping oxygen from a little bag. The first firefighter felt her neck for a pulse.

"She's arrested," he said to another man who muttered something into his radio. Then he knelt on the edge of the bed and began pumping at my mother's chest with the heels of his hands.

"Oh, God," I said, standing there helplessly. "I've killed her."

Barnard sat on his chair against the wall and didn't seem to notice the commotion.

A moment later, ambulance attendants arrived. One attendant attached another tube to the oxygen mask and started pumping medicine in. Another wheeled in a machine — the kind with paddles that shoot electric shocks to the heart. The firefighters moved to the side. One still pumped at the airbag. The ambulance attendant held the paddles over my mother. A second attendant fiddled with some knobs on the machine. Then the first put the paddles onto my mother and said, "Clear!" Her whole body shuddered against the mattress.

"Nothing," the attendant said.

"Clear!" The first attendant applied the paddles. My mother bounced on the bed again. I thought of the Bouncing Men and my father running away from us. I wasn't done with him. I still had some things to say.

I felt a hand on my shoulder.

Clare.

The little squiggly line on the heart monitor had turned into a regular mountain-range wave pattern. The attendant looked relieved. My body felt like noodles. I hadn't realized how shaky I was.

The attendant picked up the psychic phone line. They weren't giving advice. They were asking for it. They were talking to the hospital, saying something about "SPT 30 . . ." Numbers that described my mother.

"Is she all right?" I asked. I wasn't sure I wanted to hear the answer.

"We have to get her out of here," they said, looking around for another door. "How does she get out?"

"She never leaves."

"Never?"

"No."

"We'll have to cut her out. She needs to get to a hospital."

Uncle Barnard stood up. He looked like a zombie. He

stood without moving for a moment. Then he walked out of the room. I heard the front door close.

Good ol' Uncle Barnard. Always there when you need him. Guess it runs in the family.

The firefighters pulled my mother's bed away from the wall. She opened her eyes in alarm, then quickly closed them again.

"It's OK, Marcia. It's OK," Clare repeated.

One of the firefighters returned from the fire truck with something that looked like a welding torch. It was as if he was drawing on the wall, except that as he slowly moved the torch down its surface, a crack of light appeared. A little bit of the outside was getting in. It was like a Light Saber from Star Wars. It *would* take something from a galaxy far away to get my mom out of her closed-in world.

Three minutes later, the firefighter lifted his boot to the rectangle of cut-out wall and pushed. The slab of wall fell out into the driveway. A rectangle of bright gray light fell in. It made me blink. As if I'd just been rescued from a cave.

The ambulance attendants and the firefighters consulted about a stretcher.

"I don't think we'll be able to . . ."

"She's too big to . . ."

"We'll use that door," a firefighter said firmly.

In a second he had lifted the door from its hinges and laid it beside my mother's bed. They slipped some ropes under it. It took three people to roll her off the bed and onto the door. A firefighter spoke into his radio. There was the sound of an engine revving, then a whirring noise. A ladder slid through the opening in the wall and into position over my mother. They tied the ropes to the side of the ladder. It slowly lifted and my mother was raised a foot above the ground. The ladder slowly retracted and, with a firefighter on either side of her, she floated out of the bedroom.

"I'll go with them," Clare said. "We don't want anything to upset her. You can come later."

I heard the slam of the ambulance door and the sirens began again. There was the crackle of radios, more sound from the ladder. Then the fire truck drove away. Everyone had gone.

I sat down on my mother's bed. For as long as I could remember, it had never been empty. This was the first time I'd ever been home by myself.

I looked at the wall. What was I going to do about the huge hole?

thirty-three

Just Like Me

I sat for a long time in my mother's empty bedroom, thinking about everything. Eventually, I got up and went into the kitchen to make a sandwich. The phone rang. By pressing it between my ear and shoulder, I could sandwich-make and talk at the same time.

Now there's a useful skill. Maybe one day it'll be an Olympic event, and I'll win the long-distance-salami competition.

It was Annie on the phone. Her mom had called her from the hospital. And now Annie was making sure that I was OK.

"Oh, yes, I'm fine," I said. "My mother's been lying to me for twelve years and now I've given her a heart attack."

"But, Alex, my mom said she's doing well," Annie was as calm and reassuring as her mom. "I'm sure she'll be all right."

"At least until I yell at her again." I didn't actually feel as bad as I knew I sounded. "At least now I know what's going on."

We arranged to meet at Gerry's Village Restaurant. I wanted to tell her all about what I'd found out.

After I hung up the phone, my sandwich-making speed increased. I found Clare's fresh bread on the counter. I assembled a sandwich to be reckoned with in no time at all and was out the door and eating before you could say, "what about the big hole in the wall?"

Oh. Yeah.

The big hole in the wall.

I went around to the side of the house and climbed through the hole into my mother's bedroom. I dragged her mattress through the hole (the sandwich held — knife-like — between my teeth) and leaned it against the outside of the opening. It mostly covered it. I didn't expect that any burglars would try to find a way into the house behind an old mattress. Unless they'd just returned from Narnia and had carried their spoils through the back of an old cupboard.

Looking at my mother's bed-turned-wall, I wondered how long she'd be in the hospital. I wasn't sure when I'd visit her. Tonight probably. I was still angry. And not just a temporary angry. It was retroactive anger — twelve years' worth boiling inside. And now wasn't the time to share it with her.

I arrived at Gerry's before Annie. Just like the last time I was there, a man was sitting at the counter drinking coffee and reading a newspaper.

Chuck.

I sat down on the stool beside him.

"Do I know you from somewhere?"

"Alex! Good to see you. Everything OK?"

I shrugged. "It's a long story."

"Maybe I can make it longer. I went to talk to your uncle."

"You talked to Uncle Barnard?"

"For a little while. I had some questions for him." Chuck explained how he'd found Uncle Barnard's door wide open. Uncle Barnard was sitting at his kitchen table still zombie-like. "I had the feeling that he might take off, which he did in the end — he just bolted out the door. Anyway, I thought I'd lose my chance, so I leaned on him kinda hard. But like I said, he was out of it and didn't seem to notice.

"So first I asked him why Nicholas Copper and his 'associates' out West would be out to get us."

Chuck explained that — as far as he'd been able to gather from Barnard — Copper didn't want anyone nosing around about the plane crash because he was involved in covering it up. There were a few cops who had begun to investigate, but Copper had closed them down by black-mailing them. He knew that these cops were being paid to "look the other way" by some big-time drug dealers, so he threatened to expose them. And he'd beaten up another one pretty badly. "Your father was a cop for quite a few years, did you know that?"

"No." This didn't sound good.

"He wasn't involved with the dealers, but I think he'd told Copper or Barnard about them, and Copper used the information to cover up the crash. You see, Copper had helped with the building of the plane. Then it crashed and the girl . . ." Chuck's voice became soft. "You do know who she was?"

"My father told me," I said sullenly.

"Barnard thought he might." Chuck paused a moment. "I was very sorry to hear about it, Alex," he said.

He waited to make sure it was OK with me for him to go on.

Then he continued. "When she . . . your sister . . . When the plane went down, they were certain that if there was any kind of investigation, they'd be in big trouble since she was so young, and they'd actually let her fly the plane without either of them having a pilot's license. And, of course, your father being a police officer . . ."

"They didn't have a license?"

"No. And because the girl died, they could have gone to jail for a long time. Not to mention the fact that Copper, Barnard, and your father cleaned out every trace of her from the apartment. They told everyone that she was moving to the States to live with a relative. I understand that at this point your mom wasn't well, emotionally, and didn't realize what was going on around her."

"The apartment? I thought my father built our house, that we'd always lived there."

"No. It was Nicholas Copper's house. Copper took off and your mother moved in. Copper's wife stayed. She looked after you for quite a few years. Do you remember her?"

I searched my memory, but the only person I could remember was my mother. My mother the way she appeared in my dreams. A young, active, slim woman with blonde hair surrounding her face like bright light. Or else my mother in her bed, far from slim, immobile, her long dark hair spilling onto the pillow around her.

The young, thin, blonde woman in my dreams wasn't my mother. It was Nicholas Copper's wife!

"Alex," Chuck said, interrupting my thoughts. "I found this by the river with your uncle's painting."

It was the torn-out center of the frog painting. There was a pouch on the back. I opened it and found inside a photograph of a young girl.

It was Alison.

Unmistakably.

I recognized my own face. She looked just like me.

"I don't believe it . . . She . . ."

"Alex!" someone called. I took the photograph and put it quickly into my pocket.

It was Annie. She had just walked in and spotted me at the counter. She gave me one of her big smiles. I was instantly teleported to a warm, sunny beach in Maui, except that, seeing her, I knew that I belonged right where I was.

Chuck raised his eyebrows knowingly. "I've got to meet Doc Tycho at the museum soon. We should talk more about this later." He paid for his coffee, folded up his newspaper, and left.

Annie and I found a booth near the back.

"Everything will be OK with your mom," she said. "I

think she's very strong. You know, my mom got to know her a bit while you were away." Annie brushed her hair away from her eyes. "She said your mother was a mean poker player. Very good at bluffing."

"You don't know the half of it," I said.

"Matt and those guys at school are awful to make fun of her. They don't know what they're talking about."

I didn't mean to launch into it right then, but it somehow just came out. I told Annie about the plane crash, about my father leaving, about my mother getting into bed.

About Alison.

I showed her the photograph.

Annie cried. I tried hard not to.

But I wasn't successful.

She held my hand across the table. Even as it was happening, I knew it was a perfect moment.

"So what can I get you two lovebirds?" the waitress asked.

Arrgh!

It was the worst thing she could have said.

It would have been better if she'd said I had a face like a blue box.

Or the brains of a dustball.

We ordered milkshakes. A chocolate malted and a strawberry.

Annie told me that Matt had been suspended. The administration had discovered that he'd been making many kids' lives miserable. Beating them up and taunting them. After I'd whacked him on the bus, other students came forward and said what Matt and his gang had done to them. Matt had broken Aaron Ryan's nose, but Aaron hadn't wanted to say anything until my virtuoso saxophone performance.

"You'll still probably be suspended," Annie said. "The principal made this big deal about zero tolerance."

"I don't know that being suspended will be so bad. I can sleep in every day. Watch movies all afternoon in my pajamas. Stay up late giving strange advice to people who call my mom's phone line . . ."

"I hope they'll still let you do *The Wizard of Oz* concert with me. My dad will be in town. He's going to invite this saxophone player he knows."

"Well, just remember I'm there to make you look good."

"You do," she laughed and then she looked right at me with her dark black eyes.

Time stopped.

"Here are your milkshakes, lovebirds."

Time started again.

"I'll turn myself in at the principal's office tomorrow. People are starting to recognize me from the wanted posters in all the saloons."

"Alex, the dreaded sax murderer!"

"Yeah! But it really is time to get it over with. I don't plan to keep avoiding things like the rest of my family. Or run away and join a saxophone-clobbering cult. It's more painful to run than it is to just deal with it."

The next few minutes were great. Nestled in the booth, drinking our milkshakes, hardly saying a word.

Ahhh.

"My mom wondered if you'd like to come for dinner sometime soon. Maybe tomorrow tonight. If you're not at the hospital, I mean."

I said sure. I'd go to the hospital in the afternoon.

"And by the way," Annie giggled. "My dad called. He said when you put your foot in it . . ."

"I really put my foot in it. I know," I said. "At least they laughed. I'll use the door tomorrow night, I promise."

thirty-four

The Stars Only Speak of Others

I asked the volunteer at the information desk where to find my mother. "She's been transferred to a ward, dear. Floor 15A, Room 1521. Just ask at the nurses' station." She smiled kindly, like she might give me a cookie to eat on the way.

I could have used a cookie.

I'd never been in Kensington-Galileo Hospital. It was huge. Finding the right elevator took a few tries. It was beyond the row of boutiques and past the personalized teddy bear store. Just before the designer coffee booth.

And the Rent-a-Lung Emporium.

I waited for the elevator with patients, families, and people in various colors of medical clothing. Pink, green, blue, white. I couldn't tell who was a doctor, nurse, technician, orderly, or cafeteria worker. The patients and families talked in hushed tones, seriously, or quietly joking. The people in medical clothing talked loudly. I felt like I was going to meet my mother for the first time. Just like when I'd met my father, I didn't know what to expect or what we'd say.

An elevator going up arrived with a "bing" and I got on with two women in light green uniforms who were talking loudly about going to Marlene's cottage next weekend to look at the fall colors.

The doors slid open and I walked out onto the fifteenth floor. I didn't ask at the nurses' station. I could figure out where Room 1521 was on my own: the rooms on the left started at 1501 and went up by twos. I felt more and more nervous as I got closer. 1513, 1515, 1517. Some doors were open and I could see people attached to tubes and monitors. Some had family gathered around them. Some rooms had gift bags and flowers.

Damn, I thought. I should have brought something.

Here, mom, here's some chocolates. Sorry I caused you a heart attack. Here, mom, here's some flowers. Sorry I asked you about the secret that you've been hiding from me for the past twelve years.

OK, maybe not.

The double doors to room 1521 were open only a few inches. I paused before going in. I promised myself that I'd be calm. I didn't need — she didn't need — to have another attack, all that beeping of machines, nurses and doctors running in, injecting things. "Stand aside, son. Stand aside."

I pushed the doors open gingerly and walked in.

Room 1521 was some kind of common room that they'd converted for my mother. All the other rooms had single doors and one narrow bed.

Clare was reading in a chair. My mother was sleeping, tubes coming from her nose, wires attaching her to a machine that was rolling out paper marked with the mountainous lines of her body. They'd tied two beds together to hold her.

Despite this, she seemed very peaceful. They say "sleeping like a baby," and she did look moon-faced and content, tucked in beneath a yellow blanket. As if there was nothing in the world to trouble her.

Clare looked up from her book and took off her reading glasses. "She's doing fine, Alex. The doctor was just in. They'll have the results of the blood test soon. That'll indicate if there was any damage anywhere. But how are you holding up — are you all right?"

"Yes. I guess so."

"Good. They told me that they are planning to have your mother stay in rehab for a while. She will have a chance to recover, to get strong again. Strong enough to get out of bed and, eventually, to begin to take care of herself."

Clare passed me an envelope from the table beside my mom's bed. "Your mother was very anxious for you to get this. She is worried that something might happen to her before she can explain some things to you. She was awake for only a little while. She made me promise that I'd give this to you. She had it in her pocket when they brought her here. She wrote it when you went away with your uncle."

Clare stood up and closed her book. "I'll leave you

alone with her. I'm going down to the cafeteria to get some tea." She stepped carefully around my mother's bed, and smiled as she turned to close the doors behind her.

I sat down in the chair beside the bed and looked at the envelope. My mother was breathing slowly and steadily.

She sighed in her sleep. Her eyes moved back and forth behind her eyelids. She was in REM sleep. What was she dreaming about?

I opened the envelope and unfolded the letter inside.

My dearest Alex,

By now you will have found out about Alison from your father. I am sorry.

We'd planned for me to fly the plane. I was the one who'd learned to fly.

Then I had a vision. It was from the stars. I couldn't understand it at first, but then it became clear.

I told them that Alison was supposed to fly the plane. I was heartsick about it, I cried for days, but I thought it had to be.

I should have saved her. I would have fallen from the sky a hundred times to save her.

All these years I have been listening to the stars to understand, to find out why it had to be Alison, to understand why it couldn't have been me. But the stars no longer give me guidance. They only speak about others.

I couldn't tell you. I couldn't tell you how I'd failed. I dreaded the day when you might find out. When you might find your father and learn the truth. This terrible thing that took my daughter from me. That took your father from me. I couldn't bear the thought that it might take you away also. Alex, please forgive me.

I will love you always. Of all the stars, you are the most precious to me.

Mother.

"Of all the stars . . ." Never mind the stars. I'd had enough of the stars. I was angry at how she listened to them. I should have slammed them with my saxophone case. The stars were bullying her. But she chose to listen. I was getting more and more angry. A voice inside me told me to take off, to run away. I told the voice to get lost. I wasn't going to be a running Isaacson.

Just then my mother opened her eyes. "Alex," she murmured.

I quickly folded the letter back up and shoved it into my pants' pocket. Now was no time to upset her. It was important for both of us to be calm.

"Alex," my mother said again.

I leaned in close to her. "I want to get better. I want to get out of bed," she whispered.

A window broke inside me. I wasn't expecting it. There was a sudden change in air pressure like in a plane. Anger was sucked out of me. It disappeared through the window and out into the sky. The Wizard had just told me that I had a heart. And lungs. I could feel them aching, beating, breathing, gasping — whatever it was they were supposed to do when the twister had suddenly set your home back where it belonged.

"I'll. Help. You," I said, very slowly and deliberately, trying to keep myself calm. It was important to remain calm.

But it wasn't working.

So I changed the subject. "They cut a big hole in your bedroom wall, to get you out," I said quickly, "I think we should put a window there."

My mother didn't say anything, but turned to look out the window in the hospital room. It was evening and the sun was right at the bottom of the sky. The maple trees in the parking lot were broadcasting an in-depth report on the reds and yellows of fall, and we watched as squirrels made death-defying leaps from branch end to branch end. A man in a big blue car tried about a hundred and fifty times to back into a parking space, finally taking the plunge and backing into the car beside him.

"And to think, he's an ambulance driver," I joked.

We sat together silently looking out the window until my mother fell back to sleep. I crept out quietly and walked past the other patients' rooms.

A thousand people were talking at once in my head as I rode the empty elevator down to the main floor. Kids were fooling around in the revolving door and so I went out the door marked "Use Other Door." I was a rule-breaking radical and I could choose my own door.

Outside the sky was dark and the wind was throwing leaves around the sidewalk. No one was expecting me and I had a million things to think about. I decided to take my time and walk home across the city.

thirty-five

There's No Place Like . . . Now

A couple of weeks after my school suspension was over (the suspension had only been for two days), I was getting ready for *The Wizard of Oz* concert, pacing back and forth around the house trying to become calm or at least unsuper-nervous.

In a few hours, Annie and I would be climbing out of "the pits" and onto the stage to perform our big duet. I'd promised to bring a tape of it over to my mom when I went to play cards with her at the rehab. But that wasn't what was making me super-nervous. And it wasn't that the whole school would be there (though that made me regular-nervous.) It was that Annie's dad would be there. And he had invited Screwball Lacy, the famous saxophone player for Fallingstar. I was scared to play in front of

Annie's dad, but playing for Screwball Lacy would be like writing in front of Shakespeare. And that was making me super, no, ultra-nervous.

And after the concert, we were all going out to dinner. Me, Annie, her parents, and Screwball. So if the concert didn't go well, I couldn't even hide.

I opened and closed the fridge fifty times. I turned the TV on, then off. I had a drink of pop. Then I opened and closed the fridge a fifty-first time. I walked over to my mother's room and looked out of the new window that I'd had installed there. A beautiful, clear view of the driveway and the neighbor's dogs. Unfortunately, no ambulance drivers backing into parked cars for my mother and me to look at when she came home. I had another drink of pop, looked at a magazine, and then turned on my computer. I had a million new e-mails but tucked away between a message about a new John Coltrane web page and some spam about where to buy computers cheap cheap cheap, there was a message from bounce@bounce.net.

My father.

From: bounce@bounce.net
To: alexisaacson@hotmail.com
Subject: Re:bound

I once was lost but now am bound. I'm trampoline of the world because the Big B has bounded back — he's become a Bouncing Man.

I hope you will rebound this way again. If only my heart was boundless. If only I could bounce back. If only I could take it all back. I wish you'd seen me risen toward the son, rather than fallen toward the ground.

-Dadulus.

So that's where Uncle Barnard had disappeared to. He'd revved his arms into turbo chicken mode and had flown the coop to become a Bouncing Man back at the Emerald City. When things get tough, the tough get going.

Way to get going, Barnard.

Let's just say he was bouncing off AWOL.

Ugh, a little balloon above my head said. Again, the bad jokes were multiplying like a computer virus.

But they deserved each other, the two bouncers. It wasn't my fault that we didn't have a normal relationship.

It made me think of that handkerchief routine that clowns do: A clown tries to pick a handkerchief up off the ground. He reaches for it. The handkerchief moves just out of his reach. The clown takes a step toward it and bends to pick it up. The handkerchief jumps away from his fingers again. The clown moves toward it. Again the handkerchief moves. And so on and so on.

I'd wait until I felt ready.

Ready to deal with "a handkerchief" who wasn't ready to have a normal relationship with this clown. I wouldn't wait for him. I would have to be the one to take charge.

Besides, I had my own life to work out. But I knew I'd want to talk to my father again.

Eventually.

I hadn't looked for him all this time only to tell him to get lost again.

Perhaps I could get him to stop the twisted "bouncing" puns and we could actually begin to talk, even if it was only through e-mail. Though I must say, in a way, I quite liked the awful puns.

And then there was the matter of the magical appearance of a lot of money in our bank account. Enough to make sure that there would be no — um — "bouncing" checks. My mother didn't have much savings — we'd relied on the checks from the Psychic Phone Network, and since she was in the rehab she wasn't going to be working for a while. So who put the money in the bank? My father? Uncle Barnard? (After all, he had just renounced his luxurious life of lint-covered teabags and smelly fish doorknockers.)

Ha! I know.

It must have been Nicholas Copper. He'd made so much money harvesting dirt on his farm that he was bribing me not to tell anyone about his involvement in the plane crash.

Yeah, right.

I certainly wasn't planning on asking anyone to look into this or any other part of the frogplane story. It had messed up enough lives. Maybe one day I'd write it down.

You know, like Shakespeare.

But for now, I wasn't even going to finish the interview with Chuck. Not after how everything had turned out. But it was OK. Clare had said there'd be plenty of other opportunities and not to worry about it. Besides, in the last few weeks, Chuck had e-mailed me several times from whatever city he was in. He promised to take me flying next time he was in town.

My big-time reporter notebook and my student guidelines would be ready whenever he was. I hoped my mother would be ready, too. She was herself getting ready for take-off.

Well, at least from her bed.

The phone rang.

It was Annie. She was ultra-super-nervous, as well. I lay back on my mother's big bed, looked up at the blue sky, and began to talk.

Acknowledgments

Thanks to: Anne Millyard for the novel invitation and for advice along the way. My saxophone student, Alex Levy, for the name. Brian Panhuyzen (planes), Mark Inman (medical), Steve McKee (fire), Roy T. Maloney (parafoils). Kerry Schooley for early reading. Bookfriends for "list"-ening. The Hamilton War Plane Heritage Museum. David Johnston, my agent and a gent. Lynne Missen, my editor, for mighty fine word wrangling and plot roping. And Beth Bromberg-Barwin for a whole bunch of really good ideas.

I'd also like to thank bread for being good for sandwiches, my computer for only destroying one hard drive, and the semi-colon for not appearing even once in this book; except for there.